T0198946

Nobody Has to Know

JESSICA MARIE ROSS

authorHOUSE®

AuthorHouse™
1663 Liberty Drive
Bloomington, IN 47403
www.authorhouse.com
Phone: 1 (800) 839-8640

Published by AuthorHouse 10/08/2018

ISBN: 978-1-5462-6361-6 (sc)
ISBN: 978-1-5462-6360-9 (e)

Print information available on the last page.

This book is printed on acid-free paper.

Introduction

*C*heating, or infidelity, is a topic that most people have a strong opinion about. They don't want it to happen to them, and they don't want to think of themselves as the kind of person who would do it. And yet, studies show that between 30% and 60% of all married people will cheat at some point in their marriage. That's not surprising, coupled with the fact that almost half of all marriages end in divorce … and that people are more likely to be unfaithful as relationships start to deteriorate.

There are many theories about the psychology of infidelity, including a strong faction insisting that humans simply weren't meant to be monogamous. But a closer look suggests that for most couples, monogamy is both desirable and achievable … it just requires commitment, self-awareness, and work to sustain. Historically, men have been more frequently guilty of infidelity. As more and more women become financially independent, though, the gender statistics are balancing out. Any couple can be at risk of their relationship being damaged by cheating.

You may be thinking, *But that could never happen to me. And I would never do that.*

Think again!

Most cases of infidelity go undiscovered. And most cheaters don't plan to cheat … at least, not the first time. Usually, cheating happens when someone finds themselves in a circumstance where reason and logic are overwhelmed by emotion. After the first time, it's easier to justify continuing the affair. The best strategy is to avoid that first time! But how can you avoid something you don't consciously plan to do?

Paradoxically, although infidelity may not be planned, in looking back, there are often clear signs leading up to it. The trick is to practice enough awareness of self, and to pay enough attention to the health of your relationship, that you notice the signs and take corrective action before you – or your partner – end up in a situation that will end badly for everyone involved.

What are some of the signs that your relationship is at risk of infidelity? Cheating is more likely to occur when either partner:

- Is emotionally interdependent with someone else of the opposite sex
- Is around someone who is sexually interested in them
- Spends a lot of time one-on-one with someone else
- Does not feel close to or connected with their partner
- Has an "opportunity" (such as an out-of-town business trip)
- Is in a situation where inhibitions may be artificially lowered (alcohol, drugs, etc.)

All of these factors are more and more common in this day and age, when both partners in a marriage may have full-time jobs that require them to spend time with a co-worker; when people's lives tend to be so busy and frantic that making a connection is difficult; when stress leads people to unthinkingly withdraw from or take their frustrations out on a partner. Additionally, the lure of e-mail, texting, and social media can lead to emotional entanglements that don't technically seem like cheating because they don't involve physical contact, but which result in the same type of distancing and distraction from a partner.

So, if cheating isn't usually a consciously planned decision … what can you do?

You can consciously choose to strengthen your relationship by paying attention to your bond with your partner and the health of your relationship.

One mistake that nearly everyone makes in their relationship is to identify their partner as the source of their own unhappiness or discontent. Blaming a partner is often what leads you to consider other options, or daydream about being with someone else. Rather than taking the opportunity to place blame, you can learn to see those disappointments and discomforts as chances to strengthen your relationship, by identifying where you're getting off track, and proactively working to fix it. Sure, you can also fantasize about being with somebody else … but the more you do that, the more likely the consequence will be that your emotions will drive your actions when temptation is in front of you. The best way to make a good decision is to think through repercussions in advance.

An affair can be extremely exciting and romantic to

some people… but the time you invest in it could more profitably be spent in improving your marriage. Having an affair requires you to get into the habit of deceit and lies … and it can be difficult to break those habits. As Thomas Jefferson said, "Do not bite at the bait of pleasure till you know there is no hook beneath it." You don't want to end up in the position of realizing that the one who stood by you is the one you truly love … only to find that you've pushed them away.

My novel *Nobody Has to Know* deals with these themes in the fun and entertaining story of Jamie and Summer, a perfect couple whose marriage is suddenly confronted with an unexpected temptation. Although the book is quirky and enjoyable, I wanted to explore what happens when a marriage faces the threat of infidelity … and how decisions can have unexpected outcomes

*J*amie drove fifty miles from his ranch house to find the perfect store, with the perfect gift, for his perfect mom. He passed plenty of the stores along the way but none had that certain "je ne sais quoi" for him. So he kept driving until he found a unique-looking shop with a very unique name: Slick Ladies Silk. Jamie thought to himself that it would suit him just fine to get his mother a gift from there, because his mom was the "slickest" woman he had ever met. He parked around the side of the building and set the alarm.

He reached his hand out for the antique-looking doorknob, and before he could get his fingertips on it, a young woman snatched the door open. "Welcome to Slick Ladies Silk, where your lady can be the slickest!" Jamie froze; for once in his life he had no words to say, only flooded by emotions. He had never seen a smile so amazing. Her smile made the dimly lighted room shine from the beautiful glow that radiated from her. Her smile left him breathless, speechless, and still. Hers was the most beautiful smile he had ever seen.

"Sir, are you okay?" Shaking his head to snap himself out of the hold this stranger had him in, he told her he was just fine.

"My mom, I am here for my mom," Jamie said in a stammering tone.

"Oh, is she in the store somewhere? Let me help you find her," said the young girl.

"No, no, I want to get her a gift." Jamie had no idea what had happened to his social skills; after all, he was known to be a big speaker, being that he was a CEO at a topnotch marketing firm.

"Oh, for Mother, huh, well let me show you the finest silk ever." She walked slowly past him. He followed silently, as they passed by the silk dresses, and a crowd of women gathered around them. The girl stopped at a glass case. Inside the case lay the most beautifully colored silk scarves. She slid the glass door open. "Well! Here it is, our finest collection of silk!!" Jamie heard the sound of her voice and he felt the excitement from her with every word she spoke. Dazed once more, Jamie could barely look down at the scarves she was so excited to show him. *Snap out of it, Jamie*, he said to himself. *A date? She will think you are a jerk!* She stared into his eyes as she noticed he was staring into hers.

"So do you like them?" she said.

"Oh yes, very beautiful," Jamie exclaimed while gazing into her eyes and never looking down at the scarves.

"So would you like to buy one?" she asked quickly.

"Oh, no!" Jamie rubbed his head.

"No?" she asked.

"No, no, not that; it's just I think I left my wallet. I must come back another day. I'm sorry," he said while backing out of the store quickly. "Sorry," he said as he stumbled into a mannequin wearing one of the scarves. "Sorry," he said while bumping into a lady trying on a hat. "Sorry!" he said one last time softly while gazing into her eyes from across the room as his hands reached behind him, stumbling for the antique doorknob. Finally he turned and ran to the car. Pulling on the door handle, the alarm went off. The young girl ran out to see what the problem was. He had forgotten he'd set the alarm before going into the store; he looked up and saw the girl peeping from the door. Panting for air and fumbling for his keys, he disarmed the alarm. Now more embarrassed than in his entire life, Jamie jumped in his car and sped away. The girl watched the smoke from Jamie's car exhaust disappear. "Mystery guy, I wonder if he will ever come back again," she sighed as she pulled the heavy antique door closed.

Jamie drove until he saw a big park. He stopped his car on the side of the road and got out. This time he decided that he would not set the alarm. He walked past what looked to be a preschooler playing on the slides and swings, laughing and shouting. Jamie always considered himself to be as upbeat as the kids, but today he had no smiles, no joy, and no laughter. Jamie leaned against a giant apple tree, hoping that an apple would fall on his head and knock some sense back into him. Speaking out loud, "That girl must think I have serious issues. How could I act like that in front of her? You babbling, stumbling idiot!" Jamie yelled out. A mother of one of the children playing looked over and gave him a dirty look. Jamie put his head down and slowly walked back to his car. He had a long ride ahead of him to think about his mistakes.

At exactly 1:25 a.m., when Jamie was rocking in his porch swing staring at the stars and thinking about the girl's smile, two things came to his mind. He never got the girl's name, and never even got the gift for his mom. He walked into the house and into his room. Reaching deep in his pocket, Jamie pulled out his wallet from where he had known it to be the whole time and laid it on the nightstand. Flopping himself on the bed, Jamie said, "Tomorrow I will stand as a man."

Running to the phone, she grabbed it just before they hung up. "Hello, Slick Ladies Silk, Summer speaking. How can I help you?" All she heard was silence on the other end. Summer hung up the phone.

"Who was that?" her boss asked.

"I have no idea, must be the kids playing on the phone. I hear a car pulling up," she said with excitement while running to the door. She yanked it open with a big smile and bright eyes. "Welcome to Slick Ladies Silk," she blared out with excitement, but then she noticed it was a tall lady in a trench coat. Her voice faded away as she turned slowly away from the customer. Summer walked to the back of the store and started stacking boxes from this morning's delivery, preparing them to be recycled. Completely immersed in thought, Summer didn't even notice her boss barreling through the door. "Is everything okay?" Her heart nearly leapt from her as she fell slowly back into the boxes she had just finished stacking. They crashed to the ground.

"Oh! I am sorry, did I startle you?"

"I'm fine," she said in a quiet, confused voice.

"Well you sure don't seem like it today," her boss exclaimed.

"I don't know what it is. I woke up feeling like I lost my best friend. I can't shake the feeling. This feeling of emptiness has caught me off my guard. There is no need for me to feel this way. I have my health, a good job, a house, and a great family; what else do I need?" At that very moment, Jamie walked through the front door.

"There's a confused-looking fellow up front," Summer's boss said to her while peeping through the glass at the top of the back door. "It looks like everyone else out there is busy. Could you go try and help him out? It may get your mind off things."

"Yeah, okay. I will give it a shot, but I can't make any promises that I will be helpful to him. The last person I tried to help ran out of here so fast, it was as if he had seen a ghost." Picking herself up off the floor, she sighed and said, "Okay." Summer walked out of the room with her head held down. A deep voice flooded her ears, with a sweeter sound than Mid Melodies, which was her favorite nighttime music station.

"Hmmm…still glowing, but where is that smile that I remember?" Too stunned to even look up, Summer's heart started to race. A beating in her head was drowning out all other conversations. Everything for her seemed to have been going in slow motion. Taking a slow deep breath, her eyes started to rise up from the ground. A glimmer of life twinkled in her eyes as she noticed his well-buffed shoes. A shine like that must have taken him some time. Her eyes moved a little further up, catching the sight of his dark-colored, creased pants. *Hmm…very interesting*, she thought, *but with creases like that he must be married!* Moving up a little further, she noticed there was no sagging to the knees area; now she was really excited. Halfway there now… tucked-in shirt with a thick leather belt fitted to a body that makes you want to say "Amen!" Practically panting for breath now, she swallowed hard, took that leap, and finally looked up into the light brown eyes of the mystery man that was there yesterday.

"It's you," Summer said in an excited voice, as the muscles in her jawbone seemed to be possessed, forcing her to smile so hard, the dimple on the right side of her face appeared deeper. Eye to eye and smile to smile, they stood in silence gazing at one another.

"Yep it's me, if you happen to be referring to the klutz yesterday." Summer smiled slightly and looked down to the floor. "If you don't mind a stranger saying so, I don't think eyes as beautiful as yours should ever have to bow down to the floor." Summer smiled wider; normally a compliment like that would seem cheesy, but for some reason coming from him, it wasn't that bad. After hearing her boss clearing her throat, Summer snapped out of her daze.

"Well you must be back for the scarf I showed you, so follow me and we will go check them out."

"Yes, ma'am, but only on one condition."

"Condition?" she asked.

"Yes, I would love to have a name to go with this image of your face, which is engraved in my head."

"Summer! That's it," she said in a hurried voice while walking quickly past him. "Now come on and let's get to those scarves!" Summer showed Jamie the scarves, and he picked one and purchased it this time. Jamie left the store radiating with confidence, a much better feeling than last time.

For Summer, on the other hand, it was a different story. Waking up to the sun shining brightly on her face, Summer quickly snatched the covers and yanked them over her head. "Too early," she mumbled. "It's Saturday morning and the shop is closed so why can't I sleep?" With a frustrated yank, she dropped the covers back down again, just lying there now. With the sun shining in her face and her covers to her knees, Summer wondered what was keeping her mind so occupied that she could not sleep. Tossing and turning, she snatched a pillow and placed it overhead, gripping each end tightly around her ears. A muffled ring pierced straight through the pillow to her ears. "What is it now?" Now frustrated, Summer yelled out while slamming her pillow into the wall. Summer reached towards the nightstand and picked up the phone.

"Hello."

"Hi Summer."

"Oh Suzi, it's you."

"Yep, just me, your BFF. So, what's eating you; that's no way to greet your best friend. Who were you expecting anyway?"

"No one," Summer said after a big sigh. "I was just trying to sleep, that's all."

"Sorry I woke you."

"Actually, you didn't. I have been lying in bed for a while and I just can't sleep."

"Well great then! Get up, get ready, and I will pick you up in an hour. We're going out!" Suzi hung up the phone immediately, not giving Summer a chance to respond. A dial tone came across Summer's line.

She tried to call Suzi back to tell her that she was just not in the mood to hang out, but Suzi would not pick up the phone. Summer dragged herself off the bed and started preparing for whatever adventure her friend had planned for her. Suzi was a very impulsive girl that could have anything in mind. Sometimes Summer wondered how that could be her best friend when their personalities were so different. Summer put her best foot forward and managed to make it to the shower. Closing her eyes and allowing the hot water to wash over her body, she finally started to relax. Her heart rate was no longer jumpy, her pulse calmed to a steady pace; she stood there allowing the water to consume her. Now feeling extremely refreshed, she stepped out of the shower and onto her fuzzy bath mat. She went to the dryer and grabbed the first thing her hands touched, which was jean shorts that were a little more than midway of her tanned thighs. She went to her nightstand and took out a red tank top to go with her jean shorts. Hearing footsteps coming down the hall of her apartment building, Summer slipped the shirt over her head and slid her feet into some black sandals and ran to the door before Suzi could even knock.

"No. No. No," said Suzi. "You're way underdressed." Summer looked at Suzi, who was dressed in a sweater with a turtleneck.

"Me?! I'm dressed just fine, the weatherman said that it is 80 degrees outside today, did I miss something?" Summer said with one hand on her hip and a look of amazement in her eyes as she looked at Suzi's turtleneck and boots. Suzi walked to the dryer, where she knew most of Summer's clothes would still be, seeing how she hated folding clothes. She took out a pair of pants and a long-sleeved shirt and tossed them to Summer. "NO WAY! It's eighty degrees outside, I am not wearing this. Well where are we going anyway?"

"Can't tell you," Suzi said with a sharp tongue and a smile on her face. Summer took her sandals off and put on socks and sneakers.

"Okay, now I'm ready for anything you throw at me."

"Okay!" Suzi said while walking out the door. "But don't say I didn't tell you so."

"Yeah what ever, don't say that you can't have a stroke in eighty-degree weather wearing a turtleneck." They both laughed as Summer closed and locked the door. They walked to the elevator, which took them to the lobby. They walked out of the building and got into Suzi's red convertible, where she dropped the top and started the journey off right. After riding about forty miles away from home, Summer was really wondering where she was going. Ten miles later, Suzi drove up to a building that Summer had never seen before. It was one of the tallest buildings she'd ever seen and decorated like Christmas, which was very weird seeing how it was so hot outside. A devastating bright yellow light flashed repeatedly with the skating rink!

Summer yelled, "YOU'VE GOT TO BE KIDDING!"

"Oh it's easy," Suzi said as she hopped out of the car. "I have been doing it since I was eight. My dad loves it." Just walking through the doors excited Suzi and reminded her of her childhood with her dad. Summer thought the place was interesting, but boring. She sat on the sidelines watching Suzi slide around, too scared to try the ice herself. Suzi was speeding by people so fast, she was starting to irritate some of the slower learners. She skirted through to the other side of the skating rink, where she slid herself to the wall near Summer. She begged her to go rent some skates at the front of the building and step on the ice. Summer made Suzi promise to stay by her side every second she was on the ice. Summer was so nervous. She took baby steps and with Suzi's help, made it to the beginner's circle, which was filled with kids no older than eight or nine. Suzi was as excited and bubbly as ever to see Summer having a new experience on the ice. Summer, on the other hand, had mixed emotions. As the small children floated past her, she didn't know which emotion was stronger—the fear of possibly falling and breaking a leg, or the embarrassment of being the only adult in the beginner's circle. Holding tightly to Summer's arm keeping her from falling, Suzi told her not to worry about a thing and that she was right by her side.

"Hey Suzi!" a young woman called out as she was skating by. "Let's go!" she yelled. "We are about to play Speed-and-Glide, a game where you race to a certain point and slide the rest of the way using one leg."

"Yeah…wait up. I will be right there!" Suzi yelled back with excitement.

"Be right there?! What do you mean you'll be right there?" Summer spoke out with a sharp tone and wide eyes. She was consumed with both fear and panic as Suzi let go of her and started to glide away. "Wait!!" Summer yelled as her body started to tremble all over from fear, taking her mind back to when she was a young girl and feeling like she needed an adult by her side in a dangerous time as this.

"You'll be just fine!" Suzi's voice echoed from across the room. "You're in the beginner's circle." Those words meant nothing to Summer; she was still very afraid. To her, she might as well have been in the turning lane near Key West Park, which was the biggest intersection in her town. Summer stood completely still in the circle hoping the game would end soon and Suzi would come over and rescue her. Knowing that there would be no possible way for her to cross by the expert skaters while the game was in play, she stood there. Too afraid to practice in the circle alone, she wouldn't even try to take one step in fear that she would fall. She sighed deeply with such disappointment that her friend would drag her out there and leave her in a situation like that. Summer was thinking, *How could this ever be fun for me?* She had no interest in anything there and just wanted to go home. Two seconds after saying that, Summer got the breath knocked out of her. She was standing completely still when a skater that was playing the game slammed right into her from behind. She didn't even see it coming. She was hit and knocked over—by what? she had wondered while her body was plunging to the ground. To her, it felt like a Mack truck had slammed into her. Seeing how she was standing still at the time, it made the impact harder. Summer closed her eyes tightly and threw her arms out to protect her face from bashing into the ice. As she lay on the ground in a fetal position, her heart raced faster than ever before. With her eyes still closed, she decided that was it. With or without Suzi, she was going to get off of this ice. Even if she had to crawl, she was going to crawl to the wall.

"Sorry. So sorry, uhm, I got a little carried away with the game," a man said as he pushed himself up off the ice. He turned and saw a young woman balled up on the ice still too afraid to stand. Her hair was covering her face. "You're trembling," Jamie said as he placed his hand on her arm in some kind of attempt to calm her. "Again I'm sorry, please let me help you up." Summer was so afraid that the sounds in her head were very loud, and the biggest sound she heard was her own heartbeat drumming in her ears. She knew there was someone beside her, but she could barely make out what he was saying with the loud music in the rink among all the other sounds. When she felt the gentle touch on her arm, somehow she did feel a little calmer. Her heartbeat started getting slower. Her eyelids loosened ever so slightly from the death grip that she had placed them in. Finally her eyes were opened. Even though she still could not see a thing, her long dark hair had covered her entire face. With the drumming subsiding in her ears, she was finally able to hear the man clearly. "Please, please let me help you up." That voice! Summer now calmed from the initial fear of falling; she could hear it very clearly now. Still she did not move an inch. Again she heard the voice: "I'm sorry. It was very stupid of me." *Yes!* Summer said within her own head. *I know that voice.* Her eyes now blared wide open with the hair still lying across it. Still lying there, now shivering from the cold of the ice, Summer was even more afraid to move. *One more word*, she thought, *one more word for clarity.* "Okay, you really got to get off that cold ice with that thin shirt on or you will catch a cold." *That's it!! That's him!!* Summer was now thinking quickly, causing her heartbeat to pick up the pace once again, and her breath quickened from her own anxiety. The man was now pulling her by the arm to get her off the frozen ice. One hand was pulling her arm as the other gently braced her back. Now halfway off the ground, gravity was now starting to push her long hair back away from her face. Standing in the middle of the rink facing each other, staring into one another's eyes, the noisy room became silent…as if it was just the two of them. People were still speed skating in a big circle around them, but all was calm and quiet in their minds. A strange sense of peace and home flooded over both of them. Neither of them spoke a word, just stood there in silence, but it was okay. Summer was finally calm and relaxed, no longer thinking about falling and breaking her leg. Her mind had taken her away to a solid ground where the foundation would hold forever. Summer could not even explain to herself how she could feel such a way while gazing into the eyes of a man whom she had only met two other times before now. Jamie was amazed to see Summer standing there in front of him. Never before had he felt such a connection with a woman he had just met. With only two short meetings from before, Jamie felt like he could not let this woman go again without getting to know her a little bit better.

"Amazing," Jamie spoke aloud.

"I know, right. A grown woman that does not know how to skate," Summer said as she lowered her head to the ground.

"Not what I was gonna say at all. Your eyes are what amaze me," Jamie said slyly. Summer lifted up her head and smiled. "Please," Jamie said as he reached his hand out for Summer's hand. "Let me help you off of this ice until you've had a chance to calm down." She reached out her right hand to him thinking that he would take it with his left and they would skate off side by side, but he grabbed it with his right and swooped behind her, taking her other hand as well. Now standing behind her holding both hands with their fingers intertwined comfortably as if they were the missing pieces to a puzzle, he whispered in her ear, "Excuse the position, but this is the only way I can get you safely across in a crowd like this. My body can shield you from being bumped again." Summer took a deep breath and exhaled.

"It's perfectly fine," she said…"purr-fectly." With his arms wrapped around her, all of her fears were gone. Her anxiety…gone, her empty feeling that she woke up with… gone, her burden from being at the skating rink…definitely gone. She enjoyed the ride as Jamie guided her off the ice. They stepped off the ice. Jamie was thinking how he did not want to let her go. Summer was thinking how she wished he wouldn't let her go, but they did. They let go, and Jamie walked her to a table and pulled out a chair for her.

"Sit and calm your nerves. I'm gonna go up front and order you some hot chocolate. You seem very cold," he said.

"Thank you so much. I will wait right here for you to get back," Summer said with innocent smile.

"Yes, please do," Jamie replied. Jamie returned with a steaming cup of hot chocolate and placed it in front of Summer. She started reaching into her pocket and asked him how much was it. He smiled and said, "That hot chocolate was free to all the beautiful Summers in the room." Summer scrunched up her nose and shook her head in amazement of how corny he always seemed, but yet she still swooned on the inside like a teenage girl.

"Is that your way of saying you still remember my name?" Summer asked.

"Well could be, but now the question is, how can I let you know that I will never forget your name." Summer laughed at the response and for a moment, there was an awkward silence between the two. Jamie, not wanting this conversation to end quickly, asked Summer if she remembered his name. Summer, not wanting to seem too anxious, decided she'd mess with him a bit.

"Uhm…I'm not sure," Summer said, knowing good and well his name had been ringing in her ears ever since she'd matched it up with his handsome face and gentle personality. After that, Jamie didn't know what to say, 'cause he didn't want to push himself on anyone who wasn't interested. He figured if she had any interest at all, she would have made an effort to remember his name. Summer saw the blank puppy dog look on his face and decided that she'd better not play any games with this one. She didn't want him to lose interest and walk away. "Jamie…you better sit down and drink your hot chocolate, it's getting cold fast." Jamie started smiling and Summer could see the life come back to his eyes.

"Yes ma'am," he said as he quickly snatched out the seat and sat across from her. As soon as Jamie sat down, the game ended and so did the music. Now there was actually true silence in the room as they gazed into each other's eyes. But for some reason, this was not an awkward silence. The two of them were comfortable with each other.

"My mother told me that there was a thing called a comfortable silence. I said I never had one. She said when I meet a woman that I can share it with, that she will be a woman that I can spend the rest of my life with. My mother always thought about the end before the beginning. She told me that while you are young and in a relationship, the activities and excitement will keep you. But as you get older and your body is not so active, it's nice to have companionship. To have a person by your side when all is calm, when all is done, when there are no more words left to say that you had not said to one another but it's okay.

Together you stand when no one else will stand with you in the silence. A beautiful, comfortable silence that the two of you share. Yep, that's what my mom told me, and until now I had forgotten that story."

"So, what made you think of it now?" Summer asked.

"Because this is truly the first in all of my thirty-two years that I have ever experienced it—a comfortable silence I mean."

If Summer hadn't been so frozen from the cold of the icy room, she would have melted from that statement. Although the words did help her to unthaw a little. Things were going perfect. Summer's Saturday wasn't ruined after all. Finally, she was having a great time. Summer heard her name echoing through the rink. She tried hard to ignore it as she gazed into Jamie's eyes, but the sound only got closer.

"There's a lady coming up behind you," Jamie told her. She knew it was Suzi, but she still didn't turn around in hopes that she would go away, just like she did when she'd left her in the learners' circle. It was all wishful thinking, 'cause before Summer knew it, Suzi was tapping on her shoulder. Still Summer did not turn around; she closed her eyes and dropped her head to the table.

"Summer! Didn't you hear me calling you?" Suzi said in a really annoyed way. Summer wouldn't lift her head or say a word. She was still kind of angry about being left in the learners' circle after Suzi had promised to stay and help. Jamie just watched the two from across the table, still intrigued by Summer's personality and how she handled situations. "Ooookay, well I guess she ain't talking to me now," Suzi said as she directed her conversation towards Jamie. "Ten years I been knowing this girl and yet she still gives me the silent treatment when she's angry. Speaking of knowing someone, who are you, and why are you still sitting with my friend?" Jamie never got a chance to say a word before Summer popped her head up and slammed her hand down on the table.

"Suzi! How *rude!*" she yelled.

"Oh, good…you're talking to me again. Let's go, this place is dead now," Suzi remarked. Summer did not want to show out too much in front of Jamie, so she didn't tell Suzi all the things that were running across her mind, like how selfish she thought Suzi was being. Summer turned to Jamie and told him that she had to leave and hoped to run into him again one day. He told her that he wished the same thing and he hoped the next time she came to the skating rink, that she brought a safety helmet with her. Summer smiled and started walking toward the front, with her ice skates in hand so that she could return them and gather her shoes back. Jamie just sat there with a perfect view of Summer at the counter. He watched as she sat down to put on her shoes; he watched as she headed for the exit door. The second she touched the door to leave, he could watch hopelessly no more. He jumped up with his skates still on, and stumbled up to Summer as quickly as possible.

"Summer," Jamie called out. She heard and turned. Jamie really didn't know where he was going after that, but he knew that he didn't want his comfort to end.

"Yes…?" Summer replied.

"I…I…I…don't want you to have to wear a helmet when you come to a skating rink."

"What?!" a puzzled Summer replied.

"I'm a great skater. I can teach you," Jamie replied with

the first idea that popped into his head. That would keep them together a little longer. "Well, what do you say?" he said. Summer had no idea what to say. She had absolutely no interest in skating, but she definitely had plenty of interest in the man. While Summer thought in her head, that settled it…hating the skating rink, but liking the man in the skating rink, equaled skating lessons.

"Yes. I could use some lessons. I'm not sure right now when would be a good time to start."

"That's okay. Just give me your number. And I can contact you after you give it some thought."

Summer said, "No!"—which left Jamie with a blank look on his face again. Summer noticed the look of disappointment and quickly said, "No, but I will take yours." Summer's mom taught her that it wasn't always good to give your number to a strange guy no matter how attractive he was. She always iterated on the fact that she shouldn't pass up on what could be a good thing either, so ask for his phone number. Now you start the relationship off with the upper hand, and when you do call him make sure to block your number from the Caller ID. Summer's mom also taught her that a man you just met does not need to know where you live, and if you have any interest in getting to know him better then do it outside of your house. She said that in three months, you will begin to see a man's true colors. Three months is the turning point: after being around someone all of that time, their true personalities start to surface.

"Uhm…well yes, you can have my number. Here is my business card, it has my cell phone number up there and even my office number. Wait one minute and I will write my home number on the back. Jamie started fumbling around for a pen, but he didn't have one with him. Well guess I will give that to you later, but you should have no problem reaching me by my cell."

"Okay, I will be calling you later," Summer said as she took the card and turned to walk away with the confidence of a strong, independent woman. Jamie was left there in awe of how Summer just handled him. Never had he had a woman that didn't just throw themselves at his feet if he even showed them the littlest interest. Jamie was a very handsome and successful man. The way Summer withheld herself made him even more interested in her. Now he had to do the chasing, because after all, a woman is a treasure that should be found by a man. Well at least that was what Jamie's mother taught him. The sun rose and the light from it pierced through Jamie's window, causing him to wake up before his alarm went off. The first thought that popped in his head from the warmth of the sun touching his skin... was Summer. The sweet rays from Summer, the warmth that embraced his body...Summer. The smile, the laughter, the joyful times, all caused by Summer; what a perfect name for a woman such as her. *All of the ways of the season and her personality intertwine in one*, Jamie thought as he lay in bed before he even opened his eyes to begin his day. Still lying there in a dreamlike daze thinking about Summer, his alarm finally went off. He slammed his hands on the snooze button in an angry motion, for the alarm had just interrupted his sweet thought of Summer. Jamie moved on to his morning routine, which included taking a shower, getting dressed, and burning him some toast with an old-fashioned toaster oven that he refused to replace. "They just don't make them like that anymore," he said as he grabbed his extra crispy toast and headed out for work. Jamie arrived at his office with a smile on his face and his cell phone gripped tightly in his hand. All of which sparked the attention of his secretary, Layla. Layla was a pretty young girl working her way through college as a marketing secretary. She'd had a crush on Jamie ever since she started there two years ago. In the beginning, she was very eager and always jumping at Jamie every turn he made. She would constantly tell him how great he was; she even asked him out on a date once. Jamie'd thought she was a pretty girl when he first met her, but with her constantly praising him and throwing herself at him before he ever had a chance to say something to her, he was flattered, but it all turned Jamie off. He sat down with her one day and said that if she was going to continue being his secretary, she would have to become more job oriented. Layla understood and started being more reserved at work. Still, she kept her eyes and ears set on Jamie, waiting for any opening of acceptance that she could fit in.

"Good morning, Mr. Garnett," Layla said as Jamie entered the building.

"Very good morning, Layla, and how are you today? I hope you had a radiant weekend!" Layla didn't know how to respond; she was really thrown off guard by all of this extra conversation first thing in the morning by Jamie Garnett. First of all, mornings were not really his glowing point. Secondly, since the whole begging him for a date incident, Jamie tried to say as little as possible to Layla.

"I'm good, Mr. Garnett, could I get you any coffee this morning?" Layla spoke out while wondering was this her cause for acceptance, or did she have competition on the way?

"No thanks, Layla, just set the phone so all calls will go straight through to my office today." Now Layla knew for sure, no opening...no acceptance...definitely competition on the way. Normally when Layla called and told Jamie he had a phone call, he usually said take a message and he would call them later. Now he wants all calls transferred to him. *Yes*, she thought, *something is definitely up, and with a smile like that on his face it's not work.* Suspicious, Layla said, "Yes sir. I will make sure those calls go straight to you." She was very reluctant about the whole thing, because now she wouldn't even be able to screen his calls. What a busy day for Jamie: he reviewed tons of paperwork and answered every call that came through to the office. Since he was the CEO of the business, the majority of the calls were for him, and this gave him even more work to do. The smile he had in the morning had definitely drained from his face by the end of the day. He went home wondering why Summer had not called yet. The skating rink incident was Saturday, and now it was almost the end of Monday. *Maybe she will call tonight*, he hoped as he walked through the doors of his quiet home.

Sixty miles east from Jamie, Summer paced the floor in the back room of Slick Ladies Silk. She desired to call him but knew that it would be best not to seem so anxious. Sunday was such a hard day for her, she did all she could to keep busy. She cleaned her whole house, even dried her clothes and folded them, and put them inside of her dresser drawer—unlike her usual routine of leaving them in the dryer. Suzi thought it was silly, and that she should have just called him that same night she got the number, but

Summer had her reasons and her principles for waiting. Absence makes the heart grow fonder, and now she would stay on his mind a little longer. She still could not wait much longer. She didn't want him to think she just wasn't interested, so Tuesday would be the day. Three days after she got the number.

Early Tuesday morning the minute Jamie entered the office, it happened: his cell phone rang. Layla sprung to attention hoping to get as much information on Jamie's personal life as she could. Jamie looked at his Caller ID and it was a restricted number. Normally, he didn't answer restricted calls, but today he welcomed them. Jamie put on his best big-boy voice and answered his phone, saying deeply, "Hello, this is Jamie Garnett, CEO of marketing, how may I help you today?"

"You can tell me what day you are free to start my skating lessons." When he heard her voice, he became so elated that his face started to show it with a smile so radiant and bright that Layla got scared. There was silence over the phone for a few seconds, so that Jamie could compose himself and drop the smile off of his face so that he might be able to use his best deep big-boy voice again. If he had kept a smile that big while speaking, he would have sounded like a giddy schoolboy instead of the successful grown man that he was. "The skating rink will be open on Saturday so we can start your lessons then. Friday night we will need to go to dinner so that we can prepare for our lessons."

"Well, if you think that is what's best then okay. You're the teacher." Summer would have rather gone to dinner than skating anyway, so this also brought a smile to her face. Jamie asked Summer, did she live in the same town that she worked in, and she said "yes." He told her he lived about an hour away from her and asked where they should meet for dinner. Summer liked the meeting idea because she did not know him well enough yet to tell him exactly where she lived. "Some place halfway," she said. "That way we both will have only about a thirty-minute drive." By now Layla was really interested in their conversation, but Jamie walked off with his cell phone in hand and closed his office door. "All right, great idea, while I got you on the phone, let me go to my computer and search for a spot we can eat at." The two of them stayed on the phone for about forty minutes, just looking for a place to meet. Neither of them minded at all. They found it to be rather fun. They laughed and joked about some of the names of the restaurants, and finally decided to meet at a restaurant called "New Beginnings."

Friday came fast for Summer. With only ten more hours before her 6 o'clock date, she still had no clue what to wear, so she called her best friend over. Suzi came in and headed straight for the dryer to pick Summer out an outfit, and much to her surprise, the dryer was empty. She yelled out, "YOU'VE BEEN ROBBED!!" Summer asked her what she was talking about. "Empty, all empty!!"

"Don't worry, my clothes are in my bureau."

"No way, really?"

"Yes really."

"Gee, maybe you shouldn't go out with this guy. He's changing you already." Summer laughed, but Suzi stayed straight-faced, down on her knees gazing into the empty dryer with her mouth open wide.

"Snap out of it, Suzi, I really need our help here. We are going to dinner at a nice restaurant, but going by the pictures on the Internet, nothing too fancy but still very nice." Summer continued talking while throwing her clothes out on the bed to be reviewed. "Nope, shorts are definitely out," she said as she flung the pair she had in her hands to the head of the bed. "Come on, Suzi, I really need your help. What do you think?" Summer kept saying these things to Suzi, but still she would continue to talk nonstop, not really allowing Suzi to respond.

"A dress?" Summer asked. "No, no!" Summer responded to her own question. "A dress might be a bit too much for a first date. A nice pantsuit maybe? Well, what do you think of pants?" Summer, still not giving Suzi a chance to respond, immediately jumped in with a "No, he has seen me in pants three times now. And I will have to wear pants when we do the ice-skating lessons, so this is maybe my only opportunity to show him that I am a woman. Yes, a dress. Great, thanks, Suzi, for all of your help," a fast-talking Summer said as she practically pushed Suzi out of the front door with her jaw still dropped nearly to the floor. "Well, I really gotta get ready now; only nine more hours to go. See ya!" The door slammed in Suzi's astonished face.

In another town miles away, Jamie was preparing for his date. He already knew what he would wear. He was going dressy for this one. He too thought that this might be his opportunity to show her that he cleaned up rather nicely. He would wear a silk blue vest with some fancy black slacks, with no jacket to show a little bit of casualness. Jamie's big concern was what he would talk about on this date. He had plenty that he wanted to know about her, but he did not want to seem too nosey; so he wondered how to ask things. How to bring them up without being too direct, 'cause after all, he had only asked the girl out to be her skating instructor, not exactly on a date. Silly him, this meant she might have a boyfriend; he'd never even asked and now he couldn't seem to get the thought out of his head.

The drive over to New Beginnings was a smooth one for both of them. That is, thanks to their GPS systems. They both drove into the parking lot at the same time: 6 o'clock exactly. They saw each other drive in. They were forced to park three spaces away from one another due to the already parked car. Summer did not immediately jump out of the car. Slightly nervous, she bent her head down and started dawdling around in her purse for nothing in particular, but it made her seem busy instead of just plain nervous. With her head still bent, she felt the presence of Jamie on the other side of her door staring down at her. He was reaching for her door handle. She quickly unlocked the door so that he might open it for her. He opened the door and silently reached his hand out for hers, still with the smile of satisfaction upon his face. She reached out and allowed him to take her hand. Just one touch of his fingertips sent trembles of comfort all over her body. The slight nervousness was now washed away by an intense desire to be consumed by the comfort of the moment. As Summer twisted her body to get out of the car, she gently placed one leg out, causing her gorgeous black stiletto heels to click on the pavement. During this time, Jamie saw the most beautiful sight he had ever laid eyes on: a long, smooth tanned thigh that caught his eye like no other. Summer was wearing a beautiful black dress that hit just above the knees. It had on it that shook when she shook and moved when she moved as she stood completely up in those tall stiletto heels and that shimmering black dress that appeared to be made for only the curves of her body. Her hair curled and pent up with a small lock of it dangling down the right side of her face, Jamie rendered himself speechless. He knew she was a beautiful woman, but he had never quite seen her like this before. Jamie had no more smile on his face; he was just in complete and utter shock as he stared at her head to toe. Summer felt like she could read his mind, and this too did bring a smile to her face. Jamie took a deep breath and let it out hard. "For you I have no words tonight. If I said that you looked pretty that would be too simple of a statement. Even if I said you were gorgeous, the word wouldn't be strong enough, so please excuse me if I hold your hand and walk inside this restaurant in complete silence as I continually glance over at you." Summer smiled and started walking by his side, knowing that she had chosen the right outfit. As they walked in, people started to stare. The two of them were dressed like they were ready for ballroom dancing. A little old lady with gray hair walked by them and said she thought they were a fine young couple. Jamie took that as his opportunity to find out if she had a boyfriend or more, but he was thinking if he found out she did at this point, he might throw up in the middle of the restaurant right where they stood. He started off with a little laugh. "That woman thought we were a couple, what would your boyfriend think of that?"

"Boyfriend?!?" Summer said loudly.

"A husband?" Jamie poured in.

"No!! I haven't got one, or else I would never have agreed to be here with you. You don't have a girlfriend or a wife, do you?"

"Nope," Jamie responded quickly. "Well now that

that's done, let's find a table, shall we?" Summer smiled just slightly and shook her head while walking to the table. Jamie pulled the chair out for her, which was something no other date had ever done for her. Summer looked at the menu and noticed that the prices were well above what she would normally spend; Jamie was watching her eyes get big as she stared at the menu. He could tell what she was thinking and wanted to ease her mind. "For being my guest out here tonight, your dinner is on me. So please, feel free to order whatever you like. Just make sure you save room for dessert." This thought delighted Summer, and she told him that no matter how much she ate, there was always room for dessert. Jamie liked that statement because he always felt the same way.

The waitress came and they placed their orders. "While we wait for our food, let's discuss the basics for our lessons. Listen very closely to this first thing: well you can't skate freely if you don't relax, and it's almost impossible to relax if you're freezing! What in the world were you doing at the skating rink in shorts?"

"Suzi dragged me to that place and wouldn't even tell me where we were going," Summer responded with a big smile on her face. Summer told Jamie the truth: that she really had little to no interest in ice-skating, and the best part of her Saturday was when he skated into her. Summer and Jamie both had a delightful evening. They both learned that they enjoyed laughing at simple little jokes. Before the two of them had realized it, they had been sitting in the restaurant for four hours talking. Their plates had been cleared from the table, and the waitress had stopped bringing drink refills in hopes that they would get the hint and leave. The once crowded restaurant had dwindled down to just the two of them. In their amazement for each other, they hadn't even noticed until the waitress came to the table and asked if she could get them a to-go plate. When the waitress asked this, they were slightly confused seeing how they had just eaten. The two of them finally took the hint and started looking around. They both scanned the room and then glanced back at each other and busted out with laughter. The waitress really didn't know what was funny and started backing her way away from them. Jamie paid the bill and Summer insisted on leaving the tip. She placed two dollars on the table and Jamie really wanted to leave more, so he told her that he should really chip in on the tip as well. He put twenty dollars on the table and Summer's eyes got big. "A twenty!! You leave a whole twenty-dollar bill for a tip!"

"Yep. Just looking out for the hard workers of the world," Jamie said.

"But wow a whole TWENTY!!"

Jamie laughed a little and started to walk away. Summer slipped the twenty Jamie had left on the table off and into her pocket. Jamie saw her out of the corner of his eye and started to wonder about her. Summer got to the exit door and stopped.

"What's wrong?" Jamie asked.

"I'm no thief," Summer mumbled as she walked back to the table and returned the money. "But a WHOLE twenty! That's a bit much."

Jamie's wondering came to an end when he decided she wasn't a bad woman, just a little on the conservative side, he said to himself, rather than just plain cheap. Even a detail such as this Jamie enjoyed. He was getting to know all about her. Hmm, he thought, cheap but honest; I can deal with that. They left each other with joyful hearts and made plans for next Saturday. Next week, the true skating lessons would begin.

The week went by slowly for Summer since she had built up so much anticipation to see Jamie again. She parked her car outside of the skating rink and this time she was not nervous at all. She was full of excitement as she jumped out of her car quickly, closing the door as she looked around for Jamie. Jamie was nowhere in sight, and Summer started to wonder had she been stood up. She jerked her wrist up to her face angrily, so that she could view the time. She dropped her arm down and started laughing. Her anticipation had gotten her to the skating rink a whole forty-five minutes early. Summer decided to get back into the car and listen to the radio until he got there, hoping to get more of that priceless treatment from Jamie opening the door for her. Jamie arrived right as scheduled. Summer did not see him pull up but he saw her. It was much to Jamie's delight to see Summer in her car with a big smile on her face; he hoped that it had something to do with him. He sneaked up behind her because he was enjoying the sight of her lip-synching to the radio. He came up and gently tapped on her window. Slightly startled, she jumped a little and started laughing. When Jamie heard her laughter, he knew that the evening was just beginning. He opened the door for her just as she wanted. "Now that's how you dress in a room with a block of ice," Jamie told Summer as he glanced over her jeans and her sweater, which also included an attached scarf. It was fitting as could be when Jamie reached for Summer's hand and walked her into the rink. He told her that it was okay today to rent her skates, but she should really invest in her own. "When you have your own skates, there is something very comforting about it, and it gives you more confidence. Confidence is the foundation of learning to skate, along with a few basics," Jamie explained while they put on their skates. Just listening to his encouraging words was making Summer feel very confident. She was so very confident that she wanted to see even more of Mr. Jamie Garnett. They proceeded to have a great skating lesson full of slips, slides, and laughter. Summer did learn one of the basics that Jamie really wanted her to grasp. "Just relax and go with the flow"—that's what he said several times during the lesson. She was having so much fun holding Jamie's hands and looking into his eyes that the fear of falling stayed far from her mind.

The next week when Summer came back, she had her own skates and a little more confidence than the week before. She learned so much about Jamie during her lessons, and she liked all that she saw. By the third lesson, Summer had a very welcoming surprise for Jamie: her phone number. Jamie was so excited to get the number that he memorized it the very first night he got it. He called Summer that night just to test the number out. He wanted to know if she had made it home safely, he told her. The two of them ended up talking until the sun rose. They started making phone calls to each other a part of their nightly routine. After three months of skating lessons, Summer had learned so much that tonight she was going to attempt to play one of the rink games. Jamie was there with her to show her support before the game started. Tonight he would not go out with her onto the skating floor. Before she went onto the ice,

Jamie left her with a simple word of advice. "Trust your skates," he said. Summer listened to his words and realized that she was beginning to trust a lot more than her skates. He placed her hand on his shoulder as he was seated in his chair as she stood over him. "Thank you," she said with a smile of compassion on her face. Summer went out and had the best game of her life. Even though she didn't win, she was so ecstatic about just having the skating ability to be out there with them playing, and she had Jamie to thank for all of this.

Time passed and six months after Jamie met Summer, he decided that he wanted to be more than just her skating instructor. One day at the restaurant where they had their first date, New Beginnings, Jamie asked Summer to be his girlfriend, and she was delighted to say "YES."

After Summer and Jamie were dating for a few weeks, they received their first invitation for a double date. Summer was home when she got a call from Suzi. "Summer!" Suzi said in a sharp tone as soon as Summer picked up the phone line.

"Yeah, what's up?" Summer quickly replied, as she was anxious to find out more about Suzi's excitement. "I need you and Jamie to come out with me and my friend Saturday night. It's gonna be a double date—me, you, Jamie, and uhm…John…no Jake! Or is it James? Well anyway I know it starts with a J," Suzi rambled out.

"Wow, are you seriously asking me to double-date with you, when you don't even know the guy's name?!" Summer asked.

"It's important. You see, it's a blind date. My cousin met this guy and the guy had a brother, we were all going to go out together, but my cousin came down with a cold. She can't go out sneezing all over the men! I figured just because she is sick doesn't mean I have to miss out on meeting the guys. Well, the guy anyway, I did try to get my cousin's boyfriend to come along with me and Jeff, but my cousin had to start whining about her boyfriend going out on a date without her. Man! She can be selfish sometimes," Suzi told Summer with the best logic she had to offer.

"Just a suggestion, but why don't you just wait for your cousin to feel better in about a week and do it then," Summer suggested.

"This guy has never met me, I need him to see my face so I can lock him down before he meets another. You already got your man! I need one too, so please help me out with this one. You wouldn't want your best friend out at a bar all alone meeting a strange man, would you? You and Jamie can be my bodyguards. Please, just do this one little thing for me," Suzi begged.

There was silence over the phone for a short moment; the silence was broken by Summer. "Okay, I think we can do it, but I have to call and ask Jamie. He might have plans already for Saturday night."

"If you want you can give me Jamie's phone number and I will give him a call for you," Suzi mentioned.

"No, I'm good" was Summer's response before hanging up the phone and dialing up Jamie.

Ringing commenced while Summer waited on the line humming.

"Hello," Jamie answered.

"Hiya sweetie, I just got this crazy call from my crazy friend who thought it would be a good idea if we all went on a double date Saturday," Summer said, halfway thinking Jamie would not be interested in the whole idea.

"There is nothing wrong with a double date, is there? What makes you think the idea is crazy?" Jamie asked.

Okay, Summer thought to herself, *he seems to be going for the double date. I wonder how he feels about the blind date part.* "There is one thing about this double date with my friend. You see, she has never met her date. She is going to a bar to meet this dude that she has never met and she wants us to be her backup," Summer said, expecting Jamie to say something negative.

"Sounds like you have a smart friend. I would love to go so she won't have to meet him alone," was Jamie's response.

"Great, then I will see you tomorrow night," Summer said before hanging up the phone. Summer sat thinking about Jamie's response to agreeing to help her friend. She was now even more impressed with Jamie. Since they'd started dating, she found herself happier than ever. She loved having a man that supported her with such love and attention.

Saturday night came and Jamie picked Summer up from her apartment. They were on their way to the bar to meet Suzi. When they got there Suzi was already at a table waiting on them. She stood waving her arms in the air to get their attention. They walked through the crowded room and took their seats. "So where is he?" Summer asked Suzi.

"He should be here in about an hour," she responded.

"An HOUR?!" Summer yelled.

"Yeah, I asked you guys to come an hour early," she told them.

"Why in the world would you do that?" Summer asked.

Jamie jumped into the conversation. "I get it, she wanted to get here before he did so she could relax her nerves. Perfectly understandable," Jamie said as he placed his arm around Summer, hoping that she would relax.

"Yep, that sounds right," Suzi responded as she threw a hand in the air to signal the waiter to the table. At the same time, Summer took a deep breath and leaned back into Jamie's arms. Jamie was glad to see her calming down. He wondered to himself why Summer always seemed so tense around the woman that she called her best friend. It was soon time for Suzi's date to arrive. This worried Summer. She did not think it was the right time for Suzi to be meeting any men. Suzi had sat an hour in the bar, and the drinks just kept coming per her request to the waiter. Every round of drinks that came to the table, Suzi would drink them all. She begged Summer and Jamie to drink with her, but they repeatedly told her no. Jamie was never a drinker and Summer was turning over a new leaf. Regardless of their refusal, she still kept ordering drinks for all. Suzi ordered a bourbon, which happened to be Summer's old drink of choice. When the waiter arrived with the bourbon, Suzi took the drink and stood to her feet. She walked to the other side of the table where Summer and Jamie were sitting. Leaning towards Summer, Suzi said in a slightly slurred voice, "Here's your drink."

"I told you, I don't drink anymore," Summer responded.

"I know! You drink no more and no less," Suzi replied with giggles.

Suzi continued hovering over Summer with the drink, and Summer continuously refused, when a couple of local college kids got a little rowdy. They started pushing and shoving and bumped Suzi, causing the red bourbon to rise up from the glass splattering all over Summer's white blouse. Summer leapt up from the table. "Now look what you've done," she yelled. Summer turned to Jamie. "I have to go scrub this out before it stains," she said as she turned away and sped off to the bathroom. While Summer was in the bathroom, Suzi focused her attention on Jamie. Suzi took her seat at the table where she sat across from Jamie. "You must be some guy," she told him.

"Why is that?" he asked.

"It's just that I have never had this much problem with getting Summer to take a drink; but since she met you she wants to be a whole new woman," Suzi said while rolling her eyes. She slammed her hand on the table while yelling out, "Where is that waiter?!"

Suzi got up and walked to the bar. "Didn't I say keep 'em coming!" she yelled at the bartender as she flung a twenty across the bar. Summer had come out just in time to witness it all. She walked closer to Jamie, whom she saw glaring at Suzi as if he was trying to figure her out. "Sorry, my friend gets a little out of control sometimes," Summer told him.

"Maybe you could convince her that she's had enough drinks for tonight," Jamie suggested.

"I will try, but since she is already drunk, I seriously doubt she listens to me," Summer said as she started walking towards the bar to talk to Suzi.

"Summer! You came back for that bourbon!" Suzi yelled out when she saw Summer approaching her.

"No! I came to get you to calm down with the drinks. You don't need anymore," Summer yelled back.

Summer stepped up beside Suzi just as the bartender was sliding her another drink. "Thanks," Suzi said in her happiest voice as she grabbed the wine.

"No!" Summer said just as she snatched the glass from Suzi's hand, splattering even more drink onto her white blouse. "You don't want this to be the Suzi your date meets," Summer said.

"My date! Yeah! I think that is him walking through the door! He said he would be carrying a single red rose," Suzi said just as she began climbing on top of the bar.

"What are you doing?!" Summer yelled out.

"I'm just trying to get his attention, because I forgot to bring my rose," Suzi said with giggles. Now standing on top of the bar, she yelled out, "Hey! Blind date guy! I'm up here! It's me, Suzi, your date! Hey Mike, is that you?!" she continued yelling.

Her blind date saw her and immediately dropped the rose and kicked it behind him. Maybe she had not clearly noticed him, he was hoping. Suzi hopped down off the bar and bumped several people as she shoveled her way to him. "Heeeeeeeey Miiiiikkkkeee!!" Suzi said, dragging every letter out slowly.

"Uhm...my name is Mitchell," the guy responded.

"I'm sorry," Suzi said as she dropped to her knees.

Mitchell was very puzzled. "Hey it's not that bad, you can call me Mike if you want."

Suzi crawled behind Mitchell and picked up the rose he had kicked behind him. "This must be for me," she said as she rose up from the dusty floor.

"Yeah," Mitchell said hesitantly, "I must have dropped that!"

Suzi grabbed Mitchell's hand and started pulling on him. "Come on, you have to meet my friends. They have a table across the bar." She started pointing at Jamie and Summer. Summer leaned on Jamie's shoulder, covering her face in shame. "Maybe she will be too drunk to recognize us, and she might go sit with the people beside us," Summer said, making Jamie smile. Summer found her wishful thinking to be a waste when Suzi came crashing into the chair across from her. She still had Mitchell by the hand and he too came crashing to the table. "This is my best friend in the whole world, Summer; and this is her new boyfriend, Jamie. He is a great man," Suzi said as she leaned on Mitchell's shoulder. "You guys should really get to know one another." A song came on in the bar that made Suzi jump from her seat. "I love this song!!" she yelled as she stumbled over to Jamie, who was innocently sitting at the table beside his girlfriend (her best friend), grabbing him by the arm. "You've got to come and dance with me." As Jamie was being dragged from his chair, he looked back at Summer. Jamie did not want to be rude, but Summer did not mind at all. She grabbed Jamie's other arm and snatched him back to the table as she stood and yelled at Suzi, "If you want to dance, you have your OWN date right there!"

"I know, but I barely know that dude. Jamie and I have been here all night together," Suzi said as she grabbed for Jamie's arm again.

"I'm sorry, guys. Suzi don't know what she's talking about right now. You might not have noticed that, but she's had a bit too much to drink," Summer said as she took

Suzi by the arm and walked her to the bathroom. Summer splashed water on Suzi's face and yelled at her a lot more, so she could sober her up. By the time Summer and Suzi came out of the bathroom, Mitchell was gone. "Where did my date go?" Suzi whined to Jamie.

"He said he had to go home. Maybe it was some emergency," Jamie told Suzi with an attempt to soothe her. Suzi stumbled back to the table, taking Summer's seat.

"That's okay that he left," Suzi said. Then she yelled out, "MORE DRINKS FOR US! WAITER!!"

"No," Summer said as she snatched Suzi's arm out of the air as she repeatedly waved it to get the waiter's attention to bring more drinks. Summer turned to Jamie. "We need to get her home."

"No! You go home. I got my own car, and I want more drinks," Suzi whined in a childlike voice.

"Sorry, but friends don't let friends drive drunk," Summer said as she started pulling Suzi from her seat. The task of getting Suzi out of the bar and into Summer's car was a hard one, but with Jamie's help, Summer made it.

Summer was driving when Suzi unbuckled and leaned between the middle car seats trying to grab the wheel. "Why am I in your car? I can drive. Let me drive," Suzi ranted as she pulled on the wheel, causing Summer to lose balance of the car.

"STOP IT, SUZI!" Summer kept yelling as the car swerved from side to side. "Jamie! Grab her! Push her down! Do something!" Summer commanded. Jamie unbuckled himself and took hold of Suzi, placing her in her seat, buckling her as if she were a child. Suzi listened to Jamie a lot easier than she did Summer. There was something about a man that seemed to calm her.

"That smell!" Summer complained. "There are twenty more minutes to Suzi's house. I don't think I can take the odor of all those mixed drinks smacking me in the nose the entire way." Jamie laughed and suggested that they crack their windows. Suzi began singing in the backseat. The sound was not great, but Summer was just glad she kept her seat belt on this time.

"So Suzi tells me you used to be a pretty heavy drinker too," Jamie mentioned.

"No, I wouldn't say that. It was more like I would nurse one or two drinks while I watched Suzi throw them back. She always said she hated to drink alone and, well, I guess I let the peer pressure wash over me. Still, I never drank as heavy as Suzi," Summer restated. "Tell me more about yourself. So you mean to tell me, you never had a drink or two?" Summer asked him in wonderment.

"Actually, there was a time that I could say yes to that question. All the way up to my senior year in college, I honestly had never had a drink. People were always throwing drinks in my face begging me to drink, as if it was going to fulfill their need for a drink or something. I always said no, until this one night, all the college students had this huge party. I went there with this girl that practically begged me to go with her. She said she couldn't find another date. I should have found that strange in the first place, as hot as she was. I mean, well, she was nice looking but nothing compared to you," Jamie said to make sure he had not offended Summer. She smiled and they both paused a second as they noticed they could no longer hear singing. Jamie peeped in the backseat and found Suzi to be sound asleep. Jamie and Summer glanced back at Suzi and giggled a little—after all that fuss she'd made, to now be sound asleep. "Anyway, back to my story," Jamie reiterated. "After pleading with me for days, I finally agree to go with her to the party. I should have known something was up, because my friends were not asking me to drink or bringing me beers. This would have been a perfect opportunity to coax me to drink, I would think. So after about an hour or so at this party, I start to get a little thirsty. I go to the kitchen and of course the only drinks there were the punch, BIG no-no at a frat party, and alcohol. Who doesn't put sodas in the fridge for a party?? So, my only other option was a bowl of fruit sitting in the center of the table. I'm not a big fan of apples or bananas, but there were grapes and strawberries; I'M SAVED, or so I thought. I grabbed a big bunch of the grapes and popped a few strawberries in my mouth like Tic Tacs. After about twenty or so, I realize the fruit tastes a little funny, but it's fruit…harmless fruit." Summer already sees where this story is headed and begins to giggle a little. "NO! Don't laugh," as he shook his head vigorously, "I woke up in Mrs. Finkle's rose garden. I spent the next three hours pulling thorns out of places I didn't know I had. I called Mark up, one of my friends who threw the party, yelling at him and asking what did he do to me. He burst out laughing, saying 'I see you had the fruit! We soaked that fruit in gin for 48 hours before the party, and we knew that you would go for them. Why else would we not put sodas in the fridge? You got thirsty, didn't ya? And…who drinks the punch? That bowl was ALL for you, buddy!!' Then he hangs up the phone laughing at the top of his lungs. I still got scars in places because of them.

Because of that day, though, I will NEVER drink!" Summer burst into tears laughing at Jamie while he shook his head seriously in disgust from THAT memory.

"One Year Later"

Jamie paced the floors of his marketing building with anticipation, nervousness, and an overwhelming sense of desire and even a slight sense of fear. It was only a small sense of fear, but just enough for Layla to pick up on. She was much like a pit bull in that way that she could pick up the scent. It was like she could actually smell anything in his blood that might be wrong in Jamie's life. She had seen him express happiness for a year straight now. This thing really puzzled her, because even on Jamie's hard days at work, he still expressed a sense of peace. Which wouldn't be a bad thing, she thought, if he was sharing his life with her, but since he wasn't; she needed an opportunity and she knew that the way in was through Jamie's insecurities. Layla daydreamed about the day Jamie would show one sign of weakness. She eagerly anticipated that small weak spot in this armor of happiness so that she could make her move. Layla would swoop in and catch him, support him completely until he regained the ability to stand on his own again. By then, she figured he would turn and see where the support came from with astonishment that such a delicate, tender-looking thing had supported all of his weight, and then he would pull her close and embrace her. In her dreams, she imagined that he would then stay with her forever. Jamie pacing the floor like this must mean that something was wrong. Layla had hoped that this meant Jamie was trying to figure out how he would break up with Summer. Layla saw Jamie walking towards her. Her eyes widened, her breath shortened. She tossed her hair back and tilted her head to the right a little to prepare for what might be coming. Layla heard his footsteps, she heard her heart pounding, she heard the shallow breathing from her own chest. This is it, she thought, as he got even closer. In her mind, the hall kept getting longer as if even the building wanted to keep this from happening for her. Finally he landed right there in front of her. A deep breath was let out, so loud that it almost echoed through the building. Layla could feel that this was her moment. Jamie called her name and paused. Layla stood to her feet, now only two steps away from Jamie. She tilted her head to the right because she knew that Jamie's head was always tilted to the other side. She parted her lips ever so slightly and started to close her eyes when Jamie said, "Are you okay? You look a little lightheaded. Well I have good news for you; you can go home early today because I'm about to head out." This was definitely not what Layla was expecting, but he was getting off early and wanted her to leave early, so there still might be hope, she thought. So she continued the conversation, "What's going on today, Mr. Garnett, if I may ask?" Jamie started smiling, he was glad she had asked. He really needed to talk to someone about this. "I am about to propose to my girlfriend!!" Jamie blared out. Layla stood like a rock, motionless, showing no emotion, no life, then Jamie walked out the front door. She crumbled, no longer a strong sturdy rock, but a fragile cracker in a child's hand. Jamie left the building saying something, but Layla didn't know what he said after the word "propose"; everything else was a big blur. Nothing else mattered to

Layla as she sat slowly and her heart broke quickly. A few hours later, Jamie pulled up outside of Slick Lady Silks where Summer was still inside working, and not expecting him there. Her boss, on the other hand, knew that Jamie was coming because he'd called and informed her of his plan. He had to make sure that he wouldn't do anything to get Summer in trouble. Jamie was dressed in a nice black suit. He entered the building of Slick Lady Silks, and the first person he saw was Summer. He glanced at her boss standing at the back of the building with a half smile on her face, staring at them. Summer was surprised to see him all the way over in her town during his work hours. Even more interesting, he came bearing a dozen roses. "Jamie Garnett!" Summer yelled, all big-eyed and smiles. "What are you doing way in this town at this time of day?" There were three customers in the shop, all focused on his answer as if the roses he carried were for them. He stepped toward Summer and stood closely in front of her. He looked deep into her hazel eyes and made her feel like she was the only woman in the room who mattered. "18 months ago on today's date I met you here, and you talked to me with kindness; so I come here today to present to you twelve pink roses. In case you didn't know, pink roses mean 'thank you.' These are the ones I had to bring here today," he told Summer as he handed the pink roses to Summer's boss. She had moved up a lot closer so that she wouldn't miss anything. He reached for both of Summer's hands and again he said "thank you" as he leaned in and kissed her on her cheek. Right at that moment, a limousine pulled up at the front door. People started looking out the window and whispering. The limo driver came to the door and said, "Delivery for

Summer Davis," as he carried a big gift-wrapped box. Summer quickly stepped up and grabbed it, immediately ripping the box apart without even looking at the card because she already knew at this point that it was from Jamie. She pulled out a beautiful dress just her size—a long, lacy dress with a very light blue tint to it, almost looking white. She laid the dress across her body and hugged it closely as she twirled in excitement as if she was a high-school student on the way to the prom. Jamie asked her to be his date for the evening. Summer turned to look at her boss, and she smiled and nodded her head with approval. Summer ran to the back to put on the dress. When she came back out, the people in the store were still there even though their shopping was done. They stayed for the most entertainment that they had seen in a long while in a town this small. It was rare to see live excitement. They all thought she was beautiful, with her long dress flowing. She walked over to Jamie and he took her hand as they went out to the limousine, where they got in back and were driven to "New Beginnings" to have lunch. When they got there, the parking lot did not have a lot of cars out front. When they stepped through the door, the place was covered with white roses on every table. Truly a beautiful sight, Summer thought; also what an expensive sight, she thought. No one else was in the restaurant except for the team that was working. Summer looked at Jamie with delight because she knew he had arranged this. He told her this was the way he remembered it the first night they came and ate here. It seemed like no one else was around, and in the end they stayed so long that there wasn't anyone else. A waitress came up and put a dozen white roses in Jamie's hand as he had earlier prepared her to do. He again looked into Summer's eyes. "I present to you here a dozen white roses because in this place, I feel like we became best friends; and as you know, white roses represent friendship. Also, it symbolizes the innocence that I see when I'm around you and the purity that I see in your eyes." Summer sighed and melted a little on the inside. They had a great lunch, which included all of Summer's favorites that Jamie had preordered. Summer was really happy that Jamie had learned so much about her. After lunch they got back into the limo and he drove them to the skating rink. Summer was surprised to be there because it was a weekday and they were always closed until the weekend, but today it was open. Must have been more works of Jamie, Summer thought. Jamie got out of the limo and opened the door for Summer himself, rather than letting the limo driver do it. He opened the door and approached her with a jacket he had for her. They walked to the door of the rink, opened it, and went in. Blue and white balloons were placed all over the place. Blue was Summer's favorite color. No one was in the building except the supervisor, whom Jamie had paid to come and open the rink just for a short moment. The supervisor started walking toward them and reached out to Jamie a dozen red roses. Summer immediately started smiling and shaking her head. This time was slightly different from the others. Jamie held the roses and dropped down on both knees, reaching the flowers up to her as he told her how he felt. "Here I must present red roses to you, because in this place I spent so many hours falling deeper and deeper in love with you. These red roses represent my love for you." Summer looked down at Jamie and could no longer smile. Tears flowed from her eyes; to be treated in this manner was beautiful, heart-warming, and coming from a man that had treated her with much respect for well over a year now. She took the flowers from him and then he rose from two knees to only kneeling on one knee. He reached deep in his pocket and pulled out a perfectly cut diamond ring with no box, but it was no matter to Summer. When she saw that diamond, the tears dried fast and were replaced with a huge smile. Summer dropped her red roses to the ground and snatched the ring from Jamie before he could ask what was on his mind. Laughing hysterically, she placed the ring on her finger and it was a perfect fit. Jamie smiled to see her so happy. "Wait," he said as he picked the flowers up, still down on bended knee. He said, "Summer... not only do I want you in my life, I need you there. Now that I met you life would never be the same without you... will you marry me?" Her screams of "YES!!!" echoed throughout the building and this began their engagement.

"The Talk of Two Cities"

In the town of Saratoga, where Summer lived, the streets were buzzing about the news of Summer's upcoming bachelorette party. The ringing of the phone woke Martha, one of the women of the town of Saratoga. "Hello," she said, and it was the last word she said for the next 30 minutes. Her cousin from across town immediately started discussing Summer's upcoming bachelorette party, which was being held in the lobby of the Sunset Inn, a nice hotel in the area. "The lobby was packed with women," Martha's cousin said with excitement, "decorated with a beautiful blue trimmed with silver and balloons floating everywhere. She got so many presents, I know she couldn't fit all of them in her small car," Martha's cousin said with a hint of jealousy in her voice. "Hold on a minute," Martha said to her cousin. "I got an incoming call." Martha clicked over and said hello on the other end; she was greeted by Linda, her neighbor from down the street. Linda started talking so fast and so much that Martha forgot she had her cousin on the other line, but it didn't seem to matter much 'cause the conversation picked up from where Martha's cousin had left off. Linda too was rambling on about Summer's bachelorette party. Oh how she loved the finger foods and the sparkling water that was placed in the most elegant champagne glasses. When Linda got off the phone, Martha's cousin was no longer on the other line. Martha hung up the phone, looking down at the ground; she sighed slowly with the thought of conviction that she must have been the only one in town who didn't go to the party. She knew her convictions were true when her phone rang once more before she was able to sit down. Disappointed that she was unable to attend the party due to a cold, she answered her phone and engaged in yet another conversation about Summer's bachelorette party, this time speaking with an old friend from across town named Hazel. She was very interested in what she had to say. Hazel was the nosiest neighbor in town, which was why Martha liked talking to her best; unlike the others, Hazel looked for the worst in every great situation. Hazel immediately started off saying that Summer's smile didn't look sincere. She said she wondered what she was trying to hide. After all, she was marrying a stranger from out of town. When Martha got off the phone with Hazel, she had decided cold or no cold, she would definitely not miss the wedding tomorrow.

The talk of Jamie's town was that he decided he didn't want a bachelor's party. He was very happy that Summer was having a bachelorette party, because he thought she desired a special moment that was just for her. He wanted to take his last night as a single man to be alone on his porch swing and reflect back on his life before he had Summer in it. He thought all night and he heard in his head what people had said about him. "Handsome," he had heard often. "Successful": another word he'd heard many times over. Jamie was a modest man who never let any of these words go to his head. He saw himself as an average man just trying to make the most out of his life to be happy. After all of Jamie's thinking, he decided most things were good in his life but still he felt incomplete. Jamie felt that Summer was the missing piece to his puzzle. Having her in his life made him feel full, so before he laid himself to sleep, he decided that he had no doubts about marrying Summer because she made his life complete.

There was also talk that managed to enter both towns. "Summer!" Suzi yelled as she barged into Summer's house unannounced on a Saturday morning. Summer, who was in the kitchen washing dishes, shattered a glass when she heard the sound. Summer was frightened that someone was in her apartment. When Suzi heard the noise, she knew she could find Summer in the kitchen, so she headed that way. When Summer saw it was Suzi, her fear soon turned to fury.

"Suzi! What are you…? How did you get in here?!" Summer demanded to know.

"Your door was unlocked, and it was all for the best, because there was no time for knocking," Suzi told Summer as she took the dish rag out of her hand and led her to the chair. Summer thought, *note to self: always lock my door*, as Suzi was pushing her into a chair at the kitchen table.

"What's going on, Suzi?" Summer begged to know.

"First of all, stay calm, girl. You had to be sitting down for this one," Suzi announced, saying nothing else behind the statement in an attempt to build the drama.

"Suzi!" Summer yelled out while slamming her hand on the kitchen table.

"Okay, here is the deal," Suzi quickly said, in fear that if she did not speak up soon she would lose her audience. "I heard from one of my friends that their mom was in the hair salon today and your name came up."

"My name?" Summer asked with a twisted face.

"Yes, girl, YOUR name," Suzi said in an antagonizing way. "Well, my friend's mom told her that the folks at the salon were talking about your engagement."

"Oh girl, is that all?" Summer said with a relieved smile as she started to leave the table. "Everyone talks about engagements," Summer added.

"No," Suzi said as she stood up, grabbing Summer's arms and pulling her back down to her seat. "I'm not done telling you what was said." Summer snatched her arms away from Suzi and stood straight up.

"What do you have to say? Just say it!" Summer yelled as she became very ill with Suzi.

"All right, I will just tell you, but will you please sit back down first?" Suzi asked kindly. "It's for your own good." Summer rolled her eyes and sat back down. Suzi began talking. "Okay. Some folks were saying that they heard Jamie's mom say that she wished that he would just get a dog than marry you!" Suzi placed an emphasis on the word "you" and pointed at her. Summer sat in silence, just blinking and looking at Suzi. Suzi waited in silence for Summer's response. Finally Summer responded with tears rolling down her face. She never said anything out loud to Suzi about the situation. She only softly asked her to leave. Suzi did leave with an accomplished look on her face. She felt she had done the work of a good best friend. Summer stayed at the kitchen table. When she heard the door close shut, her tears multiplied. Out of all of the women in the world, she really hoped for Jamie's mother's approval. She felt if Jamie's mom didn't love her, then she would soon convince Jamie not to love her as well since Jamie and his mom were so very close.

The next day, Summer received another visitor at her house. This time she did receive a knock at the door. Summer opened the door expecting to see Suzi again. She was very surprised to see Jamie's mom standing in front of her all dressed in her Sunday's best, with a flower hat to top it off. "Mrs. Garnett," Summer stuttered. Summer wanted to say, "What are you doing here?" but instead she said, "Please come in and have a seat."

"Oh no," Mrs. Garnett responded, "I really got to be getting to church, but before I could enjoy the service, I had to come over here and clear the air."

Summer swallowed hard and said, "Yes ma'am, what's on your mind?" Summer dreaded the answer she was about to receive.

"Well, I've been doing some talking lately. I said some things around some talking women and I just wanted to explain to you what I said before you hear it and it gets all misconstrued."

"Okay," Summer said as she now swallowed even harder.

Jamie's mom closed her eyes and went into a speech. "Well, my exact words were, 'I'd rather my son get a dog than get married.' That was nothing against you at all, baby. I was just saying my son is so young to be getting married. Yes, yes I know he's in his thirties. People tell me that's a perfect age to get married. I was just thinking he would live a little more and settle down when he was about forty-five." Jamie's mom talked nonstop until she was done, leaving no room for Summer to butt in. "Again I say, nothing to do with you, dear. Now I must be getting off to church," Jamie's mom said as she walked away from the doorway she stood in, closing the door behind her without waiting to hear so much as a thank you or good-bye from Summer. Still, Summer was relieved she came over.

Fall, October 20

Guests had begun to arrive at the oldest Christian church in Summer's town. This church was said to be one hundred and twenty years old, made of stone, and took the minds of all who passed back to ancient times. Summer knew since she was a little girl that this would be the church she would someday be married in. Her grandfather used to tell stories of the church. He had married her grandmother there, just because of the old stone walls. Summer's grandfather told her that the walls represented the passage of time, and the vines growing all over the building showed the divineness of nature. Summer loved the idea of passing through the stone doors as a new bride. She figured that if it meant the passing of time, when she and her husband passed back through the doors they would be blessed with many years together. A garden also surrounded the foundation of the old stone building, placed there by the elders to entice people to be drawn into the service. The elders believed that the beauty of the garden would attract those that passed and leave them with a warm positive feeling. The outside of the building, across the doorway, had been overrun with vines along the old stone walls. The vines were better than just sticks; they were covered with little blooms of blue flowers. Most that saw them did not know what kind of flowers they were, but nevertheless, all who entered thought, *Wow, what a beautiful place to have a wedding!*

As the people crossed the threshold of the old-fashioned building on the inside, their views and opinions were totally transformed. Their eyes were averted from the ancient glories of the outside and drawn to the most eloquent modern beauty within. The wedding that Summer had been planning since she was five was all laid out for over three hundred guests to see. The spacious tall building had heads filtered upwards and mouths dropped as they gazed upon the brightly lit chandelier. The flashing blue lights in the image of hearts loomed around the ceiling, put in place just for the purpose of the wedding. As the guests' mouths closed and their eyes dropped down, they noticed the blue lace that ran from chair to chair, leaving a deep dip between each pew for people to cross over. Homemade white-laced bows were attached to every fifth chair. The bow was white and fluffy as the tail of it hung long, hitting the floor. This brought their attention to the long, rolled out blue carpet preparing for the long walk of commitment. Their eyes traveled up the long stretch of rug in this big sanctuary as they finally landed on the center of where the attention would be. They were shocked at the uniqueness of the floor layout that was made in a circle: two circles that overlapped one another so that when the bride came, she would have to step up just slightly onto the platform. Soon the wedding would begin, so the ushers came to the front and began showing everyone to their proper seats. As they sat, they still looked around in amazement at the large, beautifully decorated church. Some guests particularly liked the unity candles that were placed towards the back of the platform circle. With all now seated, the music began to play a lovely song, "Falling in Love," an instrumental played by the O'Neill Brothers projected on all of the loud speakers in the sanctuary played from a CD. It was setting a beautiful, relaxing mood to all that listened. "Falling in Love" played on as eight bridesmaids entered there with their beautifully laced blue-and-white dresses. After they gracefully entered and floated to the front of the church, then in came Suzi, the maid of honor, in her absolutely elegant navy blue ballroom style dress. The ring bearer entered and made his way up to the groom and groomsmen who were already standing up front. Two little beautiful flower girls sailed the carpet with rose petals. After they entered, the music switched to "Here Comes the Bride." People stood to their feet as Summer entered the building—in the most beautiful, traditional, white fluffy flowing dress with a train that went on for days dragging behind her. Summer took her first steps down the aisle of eternity. In her mind she feared she would fall. That would be one embarrassment she did not want to bear for the rest of her life, but she quickly pushed the thought in the back of her head. Embracing her father tightly by the arm, looking at him with a gleam of pure happiness in her eyes, she turned and looked forward towards her future and made her way down the aisle. The ceremony was being performed by Bishop Carlton, who happened to have been the same Christian bishop who'd put her mother and father together. The tension was building for Jamie and Summer as they stood in front of Bishop Carlton, about to commit their lives to each other forever. Bishop Carlton started off the ceremony by saying if anyone had just cause why these two should not be joined together in holy matrimony, speak now or forever hold your peace. All was silent for just a moment, then suddenly a small voice shot through the crowd. "STOP IT!" All were shocked. Summer turned in amazement. Soon the room was full with laughter, for it was only Summer's three-year-old cousin, who was really just trying to get away from her brother. The whole situation lightened the mood and the wedding continued.

"The couple has written vows to one another that will be read at this time," said Bishop Carlton.

Summer started the vows: "Jamie, you came into my life at a perfect time. Just when I found myself comfortable. Comfortable and bored," Summer said with a giggle. "You brought excitement, honesty, and trust. You showed me that it was okay to have someone by my side as long as we were indeed side by side, no one behind and no one in front, unless the other person needed a push as they traveled up life's hills united as one. You are that man for me. The one who supports me, uplifts me, and loves me. You allow me to shine with you, because you are that man. I vow to you to be faithful and hold only to you in sickness and in health, for richer, for poorer, until death do us part." Summer finished her vows with a softened voice, as one tear rolled on her cheek and she passed the microphone to Jamie.

Jamie was nervous, but excited. He looked at Summer. "First I have to say, you look absolutely beautiful standing there in that white wedding dress preparing to be MY bride." Summer smiled shyly. Jamie shook his head in amazement of the beauty he was witnessing, and the crowd "awed" and some pulled out handkerchiefs for their watery eyes. Jamie continued, "I vow, to my beautiful Summer-set, that I will love you forever. Through richness, I will shower you with diamonds. Through poorness, I will make your clothes with my own hands just to take care of you. Through sickness, I will be your nurse. Through health, we will shine together; and I vow to be faithful to you because you are the only woman I need. You're the only one I want, so Summer-set, please say 'I do' and be mine forever."

Bishop Carlton continued by asking "Jamie, will you take this woman to be your lawfully wedded wife?"

"I Will" was Jamie's response. Now halfway done, Bishop Carlton turned to Summer and asked her the same.

"I Do" was her response.

Bishop Carlton had Jamie kiss the bride and pronounced them man and wife. As the crowd cheered, Jamie and Summer headed for the doors of the church while everyone followed. Right across the street from the church was another part of the temple where most receptions were held. Summer ran out of the sanctuary while all along yelling for the ladies to follow her, for she was about to throw the bouquet to the next bride-to-be. Ladies swarmed the blocked-off street, which was prepared for the crossing of the wedding party. Summer, smiling and dazzling, ran through the street as her bridesmaids yelled after her to stop before she soiled the train to her beautiful white dress, but Summer did not care. Today was her happy, carefree day, she thought as she tossed the bouquet in the air and behind her. She quickly twirled around so that she might see who caught it. Out of nowhere, it seemed, a bitter but aggressive Layla pushed through the crowd and leapt through the air, falling backwards just so she could catch the bouquet. A hard fall on her back made the other ladies look at her very strange, and one word came to all of their minds: "Desperate!!" The word was written all over their faces, but Layla did not care. Angrily she caught that bouquet and angrily she thought it had to be done so that she would be Jamie's next bride— 'cause *Summer will never last as a wife*, she thought. His first wife tossing it to his second wife…fitting, she thought. But the thoughts of Layla were like no other when it came to comprehending her life. They all crossed the street with a clear view of the beautifully colored fall leaves that covered the large fields. Summer did not want the leaves raked up because she said it was a beautiful sight for a fall wedding. She immediately grabbed two handfuls of colored leaves and threw them in the air as her photographer followed her and got a perfect shot of Summer's mouth opened with a smile as colorful leaves appeared frozen in the air around her. The guests took delight in Summer's joyful bliss as she rained down on everyone with her laughter. The reception area was elegantly decorated. White lace cloths covered each table and floating candles, in a pretty blue liquid, helped dress the tables. All the dishes were in silver, including the plates. Summer liked this old-fashioned classical look. The reception was warm and joyful. The couple entertained their family and friends for the first time as a married couple. Jamie couldn't have been happier just sitting back watching Summer in the spotlight and having the time of her life. The couple had a not so restful, adventurous night at a hotel in Jamie's hometown. The next morning, they prepared to leave for their honeymoon. At 6:30 a.m., Jamie woke up to the sun warming his face. He sat up quickly in the bed with visions from the night flashing through his head with images of a high-rising beauty and an open vessel of love, eyes set in a daze and mind dwelling on the amazement of experiencing a new love for the first time. He had traveled this road before with others, but none so sweet and satisfying and filling to the fullest depths of his being. There was something about true love, he thought, and having to wait until marriage per Summer's request helped a lot with the sensation and the exploitations throughout the night as well. A rare jewel he thought Summer to be, because she was a true virgin until the honeymoon night. He was truly frustrated at times, but all along thinking the treasure was worth the hunt. Summer, being preserved and respectful to herself, made him want to respect her just as much. Shaking his body to see if he was still dreaming, his head turned to the right. A sleeping Summer beauty lay beside him, on his right-hand side; right where she should be, he thought. Forever she would stand by his right hand, leading him to higher and higher heights. All these thoughts and more dashed through his mind as he gazed upon his sleeping beauty. Popping her eyes open quickly, Summer sprung off of the bed and onto her feet. Summer asked, "Why in the world are you staring at me?" Jamie, very surprised by this reaction, started laughing. Summer, startled by the feeling of being watched, calmed down with his laughter and fell across the bed where they both tossed around laughing. That was, until Jamie tried to repeat some of the actions of the night before. Summer jumped up, running towards the bathroom yelling in laughter, "We gotta hurry and get ready or we'll miss our plane!!" The door of the bathroom slammed shut and Jamie was no longer laughing, just staring at the ceiling as his own thoughts floated him away to a very happy place. As he lay longer, he could hear the running water from Summer's shower and he imagined the hot water caressing Summer's smooth skin. The thought was too much to handle, so he got up and walked to the bathroom to join her in the shower; but when he reached for the knob and turned it, the door was locked. He knocked, but she could not hear him with the running water and her own singing. He turned away and walked to the bed, stopping there and letting all the weight his weight go as he fell face first onto the bed. After a while, Summer came out of the bathroom, fully dressed and perfumed. She noticed Jamie was still lying on the bed face down. "What are you doing?" she yelled. "We are going to be late! Please get ready!" Lifting his head slowly with a dopey look on his face, he said, "Yes, ma'am," and dragged himself to the bathroom and showered and got dressed. When Jamie came out of the bathroom, he saw Summer sitting on the edge of the bed with both hands in her lap with all of her fingers intertwined and her eyes slightly teared over. A very childlike look of innocence she held as she sat there. Jamie immediately went to her. "What's wrong?" She lifted her head high to see his face as one tear fell from her eye and down her cheek. "I have never flown before," she told him in a fearful voice. A feeling of relief came to Jamie when he found out that was why she was crying. For it was a lot better than anything he had in his mind. Jamie, not knowing what else to say, tried to calm her with conversations of the honeymoon trip.

Jamie said, "You are gonna love Europe, it is a great continent; so full of history that you could spend your whole life reading about it."

"You haven't been there before, have you? You know I only want a honeymoon that we both can experience for the first time together." Summer had a whine in her voice and puppy dog look that Jamie just found adorable.

"No ma'am!" he said with a sharp edge. "Like I said, there is so much history that you can spend your whole life reading about; and...well...so far that's what I have been doing." He smiled and touched her hand. Then he said, "Because the first viewing is something I only wanted to experience for the first time with the one I want to spend the rest of my life with, so we can sit on a porch swing when we are old and talk about Europe's great sights!!"

Summer, taking a deep sigh of relief with a faraway look in her eyes, said, "That would be nice." Jamie was feeling well accomplished for calming down his new wife. They checked out of the hotel and headed to the airport. Summer was fine on the way to the airport, but once she got there she began to get a little shaky. A plane nearby was preparing for takeoff. "Oh my goodness that noise! How can we bear the ride, with all of that noise?!" Summer screeched. Jamie started to laugh a little, then quickly straightened up his tone since he noticed her seriousness.

"Well, dear, it will not be so bad once we are on the plane. After takeoff, things will start to smooth out."

Summer stared at Jamie with a look of "yeah right" on her face. Jamie, in a strained voice from lifting the luggage, told Summer that they needed to hurry into the luggage screening area. The bags were checked and an employee told them to go to the ticket area next. He gave them instructions, but Summer was not paying much attention because she wanted her luggage. She asked Jamie to go and see where their bags were. She went to the manager and he told her that an authorized person would bring their luggage to the ticket counter so they could complete the check-in process. Summer thought this whole process was ridiculous. The man ensured her that the luggage was safe with them. Jamie reached for Summer's hand and started pulling her away in mid-sentence so the poor man behind the counter could catch a break from the confused rambling of a small-town woman who had never flown before. Even being yanked slightly down the hall Summer still aimed towards the counter boy and yelled out at him, "I heard about places like this! Don't you lose a drop of my stuff!"

Jamie walked forward, straight-faced, and tried to think of something to avert Summer's mind away from that luggage. "Hey, the arrow said the ticket counter is around this corner. We're almost there." They got the tickets all squared away and Summer was a little calmer, but then the luggage came by with a guy who said he was going to take it to the gate for them to be put on the plane. Summer noticed her new luggage had the locks broken.

"How did this happen?" she whined.

The luggage boy replied, "Sorry ma'am, the bag had to be opened and well…it was locked; so they were obligated to break them." Summer just stood and stared at him, confused, frustrated, and angry. She wasn't real sure what emotion she should go with at this point.

Jamie put his hand on her shoulder, "Yeah I should have told you, luggage that locks should be unlocked at the airport in case your bags have to be checked." Jamie nodded for the boy carrying the luggage to go on to the gate; his wife still stood there with an undecided look on her face. Jamie felt bad that he did not explain the airport policy more to her. He'd only found out in the morning that she had never flown. He feared that she really would not like what was coming next.

"Uhm, Summer," he called to her in a gentle soothing voice. "Sweetie, you're gonna need to take your earrings off."

"Why, you don't like them?!"

"Yeah, love them. Hey, I bought them, but we have to walk through a metal detector before we get on the plane; and you're gonna need to put them in a basket before walking through."

"Right, I heard about this," Summer said in a lingering tone while sucking on her teeth, making a popping sound. The metal detector went off on the person ahead of Summer and they were chosen to be searched; this frightened Summer. Her turn had arrived. She emptied her pockets, took off her shoes, and passed through. Jamie sighed from relief. He knew that if it had beeped on Summer, she might have canceled the whole honeymoon. They boarded the plane and found their seats. Jamie put the carry-on bag they had in the overhead and offered Summer the seat by the window, so she could enjoy the view. The look she had stifled him, and he slid to the window seat knowing that this plane ride was going to be longer than he'd thought. The others that were still boarding the plane glanced at Summer as they walked by. The plane had not yet begun to rise and she was already crouched down with her head between her legs and hands protecting her head. Jamie tried to calm her by rubbing her back. All were finally seated when the stewardess came to the front and gave the safety instructions. This did not ease Summer's mind at all. "Just precautions, sweetie," Jamie said as he leaned over and gave Summer a little hug. The pilot made his announcement and now the trip was about to begin. Summer's fear escalated to where it had never been before. She was knelt over and panting for air and eyes glassy from tears. Jamie handed her a piece of gum and told her to chew really hard while they were taking off until the plane leveled. He told her that it would prevent her popping ears, but there was nothing he could do about her fears. The plane rises and she chews harder, the plane rises and she rocks faster, the plane rises and she hums with no rhythm. She feels the strong force from the heavy plane rising to heights unknown to her. Flooded by emotion, she softly whispers as she rocks in a fast repetitive way, "no, no, no, no." The "no's" ending in a hum of distress. After a while of riding, things were smooth, but Summer was still too afraid to lift her head; but she did stop the moaning and rocking, which the other passengers well appreciated. Even more time of smooth sailing ride had passed and Jamie finally was able to convince her to lift her head; still not her talkative self, she sat up and rested her head on Jamie's shoulder in silence. Just that moment the plane shook a little only briefly, but long enough to set Summer off again. She screamed aloud in front of the two hundred passengers. The stewardess quickly came to her side. "Ma'am, what's wrong, are you okay?" The stewardess touched her shoulder and said it was just a little turbulence, but Summer was too far gone to follow her. She cried out loudly, "We're gonna crash!!" The passengers, now wondering if she knew something that they didn't, now were all getting anxious and swarming and talking at their seats. Stewardess: "NO, No, everyone, it was only a little turbulence, we're stable now. No crashing!" Angrily the stewardess looked at Jamie as if to say "please control your wife."

The stewardess apologizing for the turbulence brought Summer a complimentary cup of French cappuccino, which happened to be Summer's favorite so she took it and sipped quickly. After a couple of minutes drinking Summer fell asleep balled up in Jamie's arms. The stewardess walked past and saw this. She had a look mixed with excitement, delight, and peace on her face. Jamie couldn't help notice her joy and sense of accomplishment. He wondered what was in that cappuccino. Jamie and the stewardess made eye contact and they both smiled, for Jamie also had a small bit of relief knowing that his dear, frantic wife was sound asleep.

Hours later their flight came to an end and the plane landed at their destination. Summer and Jamie Garnett were in Rome! The first spot for Jamie's perfectly planned three-month honeymoon. Three months equaled the viewing of three different beautiful cities in Europe. This honeymoon he had planned when he was fifteen years old. He'd always fantasized about Europe's culture and wanted to share it with his soul mate. When Summer found out about his plans she definitely had no complaints. She did wonder, however, if it was affordable, but before she could even speak of money Jamie told her he'd started saving for this honeymoon when he was eighteen years old. He held a special savings account just for that moment. Some that knew about it thought he was crazy but his mom thought, Wow, handsome, thoughtful, plans in advance, and is about his business—what a great husband he will make one day.

The stewardess started to make her announcements on how the passengers should exit the plane and this startled Summer, waking her up completely. Jamie looked over, smiling at her. "Rise and shine, my Summer, we made it here." "We are here?" Summer asked with squinted eyes and a raised eyebrow. "Yes ma'am!" Summer stood and stumbled a bit, knocking her back to her seat. With her arm flopping across Jamie's lap she laughed and said, "Too much trembling, I guess now I'm weak in the knees." Jamie lifted her hand and kissed it softly as he looked her directly in her eyes and said, "You can always hold on to me." Just from one quick landing of a plane, Summer's mind was calmed again and she no longer had the feeling that her heart was trying to escape from her chest to regain safety on land. Now it was all settled again and oozing with thoughts of her husband's corny love gestures and his sweet smelling aroma that melted her heart.

Jamie, walking in front of Summer off the plane, was carrying their carry-on bag in his right hand and his left was directly behind him, holding his wife's hand as they stepped off the plane in a line. "Oh my goodness!" Summer yelled out while they walked to claim their luggage. Jamie, not knowing what was wrong, immediately stopped and started looking around in defense mode as if he was a bear prepared to protect his cub. "What's wrong?" he yelled back. Summer responded with bright eyes and all the excitement she could muster up: "We are in Rome! This is Rome's airport! This is the Rome's floor, which they walk on," she said while flinging her arms out downward to the floor. Jamie smiled while rolling his eyes and shaking his head and began his steps again. In his mind he thought, The childlike innocence of my thirty-year-old wife is going to keep me alive forever. The couple retrieved their luggage and entered a cab, which was prepared to take them to their hotel.

The ride across town took Jamie inside to his own inner child; he gazed out of the window and every passing glance amazed him with the beauty of Rome. He was only thinking to himself now, during the whole ride, because he was trapped by emotion. For years he had studied and seen pictures, but the true vision of the place was no comparison.

Jamie's thoughts: Rome is not a place that can be described in a few words. It was an elegance that stands alone, and can never completely be contained by one's human eye.

While Jamie was completely immersed in thought staring out of his window, his wife spoke with excitement about everything she saw. Every passing item became a conversation piece. Jamie was not listening, but it was no matter for she never noticed. She talked nonstop until they arrived at the hotel where they would be spending the next month.

Rome's Marriott Grand Hotel. When the cab pulled up to this gorgeous sight, even Summer Garnett was rendered speechless! This beautiful yet affordable hotel had looked nothing like she had expected. The place was completely different from their little hometown hotels. It held an appearance of a bit of ancient bliss on the inside, Summer thought. One step on the inside and Summer knew that Rome was still with the modern times. It was so spacious and clean she felt like a queen. As she glided up the grand staircase that curved as you walked, her mind traveled back to when she was young and pretending to be a princess, with long streaming hair walking through a beautiful place just like all the sites in Rome. Finally after a long slow walk, they made it to their presidential suite. Jamie stood and viewed the room. He smiled and repeatedly nodded his head in acceptance, as his wife twirled around the suite like she had entered a land of her own. They both had a shower and washed away the intensity of their travel. Even though Summer had a long nap on the plane ride, still she was exhausted. She lay across the bed with the fluffy white comforter and the plumpest soft pillows. She sank into a peaceful position that she dared not move from, for she had never felt such a comfort from a bed before in her life. Just before her eyelids dropped completely, she began to dream that she was drifting away from all worries on a fluffy white cloud.

While Summer slept, Jamie decided to walk around and tour the hotel. He discovered a restaurant located inside the hotel. He had planned to take Summer there for dinner when she woke up. Jamie walked around the hotel enjoying the sights for almost two hours. The sun had begun to go down, so he figured he'd better go and wake up Summer so that she might prepare for dinner. Jamie slid his card into the lock and it lit up green, allowing him to push the door open. He looked around halfway thinking his wife would be twirling around the room somewhere, but his eyes landed on her lying across the bed still sound asleep. "Rise and shine, Sunshine," Jamie said in a firm-toned voice, which woke Summer up with ease. She opened her eyes and sat up Indian style in the middle of the bed. She stretched both arms out to the ceiling and forced out a hello to Jamie that came in the form of a yawn. She dropped her hands to her sides and sighed with a tone of realization. "So what have you been doing while I rested?" she asked. "I had a nice walk around the hotel. I found a restaurant downstairs. Food menu looks good."

"Great, because I am starving! I'm gonna freshen up, then we can go straight to dinner," Summer blared out while running to the bathroom and slamming the door behind her. Dinner was enjoyable for both of them. After Jamie finished a big helping of chicken parmigiana, he could hardly keep his eyes open at the table. Summer felt sorry for him and told him he should have a nap. Then they could have stayed up all night together because she was wide open and ready for fun. He told her maybe she should have stayed awake, then she would have been able to sleep at night. This statement made her roll her eyes up to the ceiling in a "whatever" type of way. "Are you rolling your eyes at me, lady?" Jamie said in a slightly playful, but extremely tired droopy voice. Summer responded by putting one finger in the air to get the waitress's attention, so they could get the check. Jamie: "No, what are you doing?" Summer: "I can see that you really need to go to bed, so we can cut this short and I will have dessert tomorrow." Jamie, with drooping eyelids and the most dragging tone known to man, reached his hand across the table, placing his hand on top of Summer's, and said, "No, we can stay here. I will wake up, I promise." Summer looked into his jet-lagged, bloodshot eyes and smiled while saying softly, "Don't make promises you can't keep." They paid for their meal and went back to their room. Jamie had a quick shower and then went straight to sleep. Summer decided she would tour the hotel just as Jamie had done earlier. She walked around slowly for a couple of hours just enjoying the view and being very entertained by the Roman accents that echoed through her ears as people passed her. Not knowing a word most of them were speaking, because the languages were not her own, but the accents still flowed sweetly through her ears. Walking forward, yet still looking behind her; captivated by a Roman couple who had just walked by her, joined together with only their pinky fingers looped to one another. They were both dressed as if they had just attended a ball that was done just in their honor. The woman had a silk black dress on that held tightly to all of her curves, but then flowed freely just before hitting her knees, causing the dress to bounce with flair only at the bottom while the top held its form. The man had a tuxedo on that was equally attractive. Summer continued staring at them from behind until her walk was interrupted by a thump of pressure that eliminated her open space. She snapped her neck forward quickly to see what the disturbance was. At first, all she could see was her long flowing hair slapping her in the face. She had walked right into a man that was backing out of the door of his hotel room. Summer repeatedly apologized, but the man didn't understand a word. He too was apologizing to Summer in a sharp, uplifted voice that alarmed Summer because she also could not understand him because he was speaking French. She quickly maneuvered herself around him and made her way back to her room door. The cracking of the door woke

Jamie. He peeped his head up as Summer stepped inside. "Did you have a nice walk?" Jamie asked while yawning. Summer paused and thought, still a little nervous from the walking accident. She said, "Yes I did, for the most part. But next time I think we should walk together." Jamie grabbed the remote that lay on his nightstand and flicked on a movie. He opened his arms up for his new bride to come and join him, so she walked over and gently placed her curled-up body in his arm and they watched the movie together. By the time the credits rolled at the end of the movie, they both lay comfortably against one another, sound asleep. It was truly a beautiful moment until Summer was rudely awakened by a dreadful sound that came from just above her head. She woke without moving, only popping her eyes open. When she heard the sound again, she lifted her eyes upward. The only thing that was above her head was Jamie. Jamie? She thought, is that dreadful sound coming from you, my love? Then the awful sound alarmed again and she sat completely still, only rolling her eyes and completely shutting them with complete assurance now of what the annoying sound was. My husband snores, she thought, OH NO!! I will never sleep again. Slipping her body slowly away from his, careful not to wake him, she grabbed the throw blanket that lay at the foot of the bed and tiptoed to the front room of their presidential suite, which had a living area set up. Summer could sleep to most anything, but snoring just wasn't one of those things. She lay across the couch and continued her rest there, for she was just far enough away that she could tune out Jamie's highly annoying body sounds. Early that morning, Jamie awoke, completely refreshed but slightly confused because his wife was not lying beside him. He stepped off the bed.

He sprung out of bed with the energy of a two-year-old. He entered into the living area of their suite and saw his wife lying there. My wife sleepwalks, he thought, OH NO!! I will never sleep again. "Rise and shine, Summer." She woke immediately, looking not so rested. "What are you doing out here?" he asked. Summer popped both eyes open and squinted them down, dragging herself off the couch. Her hair was wild from the tossing and turning of the night. She combed it away from her face with her fingers, tossing her long hair back as she stood to her feet and looked him in his eyes. Summer said with a little frustration, "Why didn't you tell me?" With a puzzled face, Jamie asked her what she could possibly be talking about. "The snoring," Summer said simply with a slight attitude, with one eyebrow raised and widened eyes. Jamie was shocked to even hear that he snored. He had never heard it told before. "I snore?" he said with a surprised look. Guess that's what happened in the middle of the night, he thought. Summer just stared blankly with no response and dragged her body, frizzy hair, and sloppy attire to the bathroom, where she slammed the door behind her. Jamie stood there for a second wondering why she always slammed the bathroom door, then he yelled, "I was VERY tired, that can cause temporary snoring spells… YOU KNOW!!" He still got no response from Summer. Twenty minutes later, Summer ran out of the bathroom screaming with excitement, dripping wet with only a towel wrapped around her. She began twirling around the suite again. Jamie just stood and stared at her with his nose scrunched up and eyebrows knitted close together, now more confused than ever. That bathroom works miracles, he thought, in one way or another. He sighed deeply as he stared at her twirl, shaking his head with a smile. No! he thought, it's just my wife's amazing personality. Summer ran up to him and jumped into his arms. "ROME!" she yelled. "We are still in Rome! Rome, I almost forgot. This is gonna be our first real day in Rome!"

"Yeah, we had our rest day. Now, the town is ours! I have a surprise for you. One of the wedding gifts I received from my guys at the marketing firm was our very own personal tour guide of Rome! They all chipped in to pay for this guy and I heard he was great. He lives here and speaks perfect English. He will take us around and explain the history of the places he shows us. He's supposed to be here in about an hour to pick us up." Summer hopped out of his arms and ran for her suitcase. "One hour?! There is not enough time," she yelled as she flung clothes across the room in a panic. Jamie walked behind her picking up every item and folding it back again. Soon they were both dressed and waiting at the front entrance for their travel guide, Jaqua, to come for them. He arrived in one of the finest custom-made suits with a white shirt and a poppingly dashing bow tie. His attire shamed both Summer and Jamie, who were simply wearing causal clothing for the evening. "I am Jaqua, your very expensive, pardon, I mean your very experienced travel guide," he corrected himself with his strong accent. "We are first to tour the Capitoline Museum." They arrived to the museum and Jaqua shared much about it with them.

Jaqua: "The Capitoline Museum has two parts to it, Palazzo Nuovo and Palazzo Nuovo first and some fascinating Greek and Roman sculptures." Next they admired Palazzo Dei Conservatori, where the halls were colorful and the building was filled with fabulous paintings by Tintoretto,

Veronese, and Caravaggio. Summer was rather bored with the whole museum experience but dared not share that information with Jamie, who appeared to have been in his own personal heaven. When Jamie thought of Europe, the first thing that popped in his head was museums. When Summer thought of Europe, shopping stores were what floated in her head.

When they exited the building, Jaqua left them for the evening. He promised that he would return tomorrow. Jamie's mind was captivated by all that he had seen and heard inside the museum. Summer was ready for excitement. The two of them had opted to walk the streets of Rome instead of catching a ride back to the hotel with Jaqua. This way they could enjoy some sights. The two of them stood on the pavement outside the museum as bicyclists and other tourists passed by them with shopping bags and dressed from anything to stylish cut-off jeans with long sleeves but cut off right before the belly button, and some had fancy tailor-made dresses that fit their bodies like a well-knitted glove. Summer stood with a panting look while searching for adventure. Much like a hunting dog. Jamie stood with a content, settled-type look as if he could have rolled over and took a nap after an exciting night. Summer suddenly slandered that, though, before it even came into existence. She stooped gazing out at the crowd and she snatched her head in Jamie's direction with a big smile and bright eyes that he could never resist. She said, "Let's go ski boat riding!" He just stared at her for a moment, choosing his words wisely before he spoke. He had grown to know that his wife was very sensitive. "Uhm…ski boat riding? In Rome?"

"Yeah, there are beaches and ski boats in Rome you

know. It will be fun," she responded. "Yes, this is true, but ski boat riding in October?" he questioned.

"Yep, makes for even more excitement when the water splashes you and you get that fall breeze chilling your body. It is still early. Not too cold out," Summer said while sliding her hand on the inside of Jamie's black leather coat, reaching for his phone. He always kept his phone on the inside pocket of his coat while he was out. She grabbed the phone and placed it in his hand. "Here, call Jaqua back and ask him where we go to find the nearest beach." Hesitantly, Jamie dialed and the phone began to ring. Now on its fourth ring there was still no answer, and Jamie was still no answer. Jamie was getting relieved and he raised a finger to turn off the phone, and just before the tip of his nail could reach the disconnect button he heard a hello. Summer was relieved and Jamie was slightly disappointed.

They walked to a little lunching area nearby where they sat at one of the tables outside and ate while they waited on Jaqua, who was nice enough to pick them up and drive them to the beach. The smell of the saltwater filled the air. Only a few summer stragglers walked the beach; others decided it was just too cold for beach fun. This beach had a man that sat in a lounge chair under a wooden tent. He had this area so he could provide activities to the guests, and as Jaqua was approaching the tent they noticed the man lying there in his lounge chair with his legs crossed over each other at the angle and a straw hat lying across his face. The rapid rising of his belly gave all the appearance that he was sleep. The man was surrounded by activities such as beach balls, a valley ball net, and many other fun beach items, but the main ingredients that Summer saw were two ski jets that sparkled white from the gleaming of the sun. Jaqua cleared his throat as they took their final steps to the tent and attempted to wake the resting man from his nap. Still the man slept on. Jaqua said "excuse me, sir" in his fine Italian accent. Startled for a moment, the man's hand flew up a moment as he reached for his straw hat to remove it from his face. He accidentally knocked it to the and reaching for it caused him to flip over on the sand with the lounge chair draped across him. Summer giggled a little in the background. Jamie rushed to remove the lounge chair from the man's body. "Good evening," the half-asleep man said as he rose from the ground dusting the sand out of his hat. "How can I help you today?" the man finally asked. Jaqua quickly spoke and asked the man for details on ski boat riding. They could choose to ride for thirty minutes or an hour. Both for a reasonable price. Jaqua looked back at Jamie for him to choose a time and Jamie turned and looked at Summer. Summer, in turn, blurted out, "An hour will do just fine."

They had a blast on the ride and Jamie was shocked when Summer zoomed past and cut across him like a pro ski rider. This caused spurts of water to dash on him. Summer had found a skill that she did not know she possessed. She was a great ski rider. Summer circled around and came up behind Jamie, since he was practically sitting still, in admiration of what he had seen. She sped beside him yelling, "Let's go, slowpoke," and so he did. They raced around that whole hour. Jamie ended up so motivated by the chase, he forgot all about how cold he was. They both appeared back on the sand sloppy wet from being splashed. The activity man sold them two big beach towels to wrap around them for the ride back to the hotel so they would not damage Jaqua's grey suede seats, which he adored. Jamie and Summer were both so exhausted, they were quiet for the whole ride. They arrived back at the hotel. Even though it was only 6:30 they washed up and went straight to bed, skipping dinner. Jamie was so tired he snored louder than the night before, but it was okay because Summer was too tired to wake up and hear him.

When they woke up they were both feeling good, but tired. As they lay in bed side by side, Summer shared a dream with Jamie: "Last night I had the greatest dream. We moved to Rome. All of our family and friends got so jealous that they also moved to Rome. When they came, everything was perfect. Not that it was not perfect when it was just the two of us, but family does make things complete. Well anyway," Summer said after rambling on, "it was a perfect dream for a perfect night."

"My dream was quite the opposite of yours," Jamie spoke out. "It was not so perfect. In fact it was weird, confusing, and hurtful. I was glad when I woke from it," Jamie told her.

"Wow, tell me about it," she asked of him.

"A dream like that I don't usually want to say out loud, but I will tell you a small part. In the dream, I lost you; and I spent the rest of my life searching for you. I never found you, but I never stopped loving you." Jamie lowered his head in sorrow after sharing his dream. Summer leaned in closer and rested her head on his chest, as he lay flat on his back. "You will never lose me," she assured him. "I am too clingy to ever get lost." They chuckled together and started getting out of the bed so that they could prepare for their day. After they got dressed they were undecided what they wanted to do for the day. They ended up going to a movie. After the movie they stopped in to eat at an interesting restaurant which served Italian dishes that they were not familiar with.

When they entered the restaurant the food smelled delicious, and they sat somewhere in the middle of the almost packed restaurant. It was the only table they could find open.

"All right, we gotta do the thing," Jamie popped out of his mouth. "The *thing*?" Summer responded with a questioning tone.

"Yeah, the thing," he replied once more.

"What thing?" she bluntly asked. "The thing that we said we were going to do in every state that we traveled to on our honeymoon!" he responded. "Oh ooooooooooo that thing," Summer said with widened eyes and a dropped jaw, just before she busted out in laughter, shaking her head vigorously as she pleaded out aloud. "It was on a television show we were watching, Jamie," she spoke to him.

"Yeah but that guy was enjoying some interesting out-of-state cuisines," he replied.

"Yuck," was her reply. "One state had him eating a cow's tongue," Summer said in disgust. Jamie chuckled a bit before saying, "Yeah but looked like he was really enjoying it, and besides you lost a bet that night. Remember? You promised to take the punishment of going to one restaurant in every state that we ever travel to and try their oddest dish on the menu. "Yeah but…," Summer said and paused. Jamie jumped in with "and I promised to share your punishment and take a bite myself. Your word is your bond. Now let's start this marriage out right," he said. With a slight look of fear on her face she said, "Okay, yeah I will do it."

"Great then! Let's check the menu." Everything was written in Italian so they decided just to call the waiter over and ask him what the most exotic thing on the menu was. He stated, "Casu Marzu," which neither Summer or Jamie had any idea what it meant, but agreed to order it just the same. When the waiter brought the order and placed it on the table, it had a stench of an unclean baby. The smell hit all of their noses hard. Before they could ask, the waiter immediately explained the dish. "Casu Marzu in English means 'rotten cheese.'" When the waiter said this, Summer popped her eyes open wide and frowned. The waiter continued talking. "It is fermented sheep filled with the larvae of a kind of fly. In other places it is also called 'maggot cheese.'" As soon as the words "maggot cheese" popped out of his mouth Summer clenched her mouth shut and slammed her hand on the table and used it to push her seat far away from the plate. "No, not gonna happen," she said. "Your word is your bond," Jamie told her again. Somehow this meant something to Summer and she decided to do it. Picking up the cheese with her fork in her right hand and pinching her nose shut with her left, she raised the fork higher. As she gazed at the cheese something appeared to be popping, and she dared not ask what. Squeezing her nose tighter she quickly shuffled the cheese in, swallowing it hard with no chewing. It was her biggest attempt possible to bypass her tongue. After she had done it she sat quietly and it was Jamie's turn. He swallowed a piece with ease and even had another bite. The waiter who had stood over them watching the whole thing said to him in his strong Italian accent, "Yes, yes, eat quickly, this meal has to be eaten when the maggots are alive or the meal goes bad." A straight-faced

Summer, who had not said a word since she had her bite, never looked up at the waiter when he said this, but she heard him loud and clear. She slung her head to the side of her chair and violently vomited on the restaurant floor with several disturbed guests watching. Jamie, who was extremely sorry he had pushed the issue, got his wife back to the hotel and all cleaned up, but every time she thought of eating live maggots she leapt out of the bed running towards the bathroom slamming the door behind her. Continually she did this and vomited all through the night. Jamie lay on his back on top of the bed comforter and thought to himself as Summer was in the bathroom sick, Well, I guess it is not a good idea to try and force someone to do anything, bet or no bet.

When the sun rose Summer lay still all curled up on the couch that was closest to the bathroom door. Finally her stomach was settled, her mind was settled, and she was sound asleep. Jamie woke with the rising sun and wrapped Summer with a blanket as easily and gently as possible so as not to wake her. He eased out the door quietly and went down to the hotel lobby, where he had his breakfast alone. Not wanting to wake Summer, Jamie sat around the lobby reading magazines one after another. Soon noon came, and Jamie's face was buried in his eight magazines when he heard the clicking of high heels getting louder. Then suddenly the clicking stopped. Still holding the magazine to his face, his eyes dropped to the white-tiled floor where he noticed the black high heels had approached him and came to a complete halt. He dropped the magazine and raised his eyes slowly from heels to knees and hips to the rest until he saw the face of his wife. She was standing in front of him quietly. He pushed the magazine aside and stood to his feet in front of her. He took both of her hands in his and leaned over, kissing her gently on the cheek. With no words all hard feelings were gone and the two of them walked out of the hotel together hand and hand. They had a great day touring Rome.

Time had passed and Thanksgiving had arrived. It also happened to be their last night in Rome. Summer and Jamie both woke up early on Thanksgiving day. Since it was their last day in London they wanted to prepare for their early morning departure. They spent their day packing and snacking on whatever they could get their hands on. Summer leaned over her suitcase, which lay on her bed. She pressed down hard with her arms and still it did not snap shut. "Every city we leave makes packing harder and harder," Summer stated in a strained voice as she pressed down repeatedly on the suitcase. "Well maybe we should cut out all the shopping trips," Jamie said as he walked over and used his manly strength to press the suitcase shut. Summer slapped herself on the bed after seeing Jamie accomplish closing the suitcase with ease after all her hard work. Yes, she thought to herself, having a husband will come in handy. She lay on her back and sighed as she rested from her busy morning. "No! We can't shop less. We will just have to buy more suitcases," Summer said with a very delayed response. Jamie smiled and continued packing. A few minutes later Summer saw Jamie bagging up all of the snack food. She hopped off of the bed and grabbed a bag of chips from his hand before he had time to bag them. He watched her as she ripped the bag open and began shuffling chip after chip into her already full mouth. "Starved are we?" he asked her jokingly. "It's Thanksgiving and we spent all day working," Summer mumbled out while still munching on her chips. After swallowing she continued speaking, "Chips and cookies are great but they are no turkey and sweet-potato pie." "Well, I have a great idea," Jamie announced. "Oh yeah, do tell," Summer spoke out as he piqued her interest. "We will finish packing everything, clean up a little…" "You're losing me," Summer jumped in and said before he was done speaking.

"How?" he stopped and asked. "I haven't even got to the good part yet."

"Oh, sorry, it's just you said clean up a little. After we pack all of our stuff we don't have to clean. This is a hotel, there is maid service," she told him.

"Still I like to tightly what I can just to help out," Jamie said to her. "You really are a perfect man," Summer said out loud while really thinking, You really are a neat freak!

"But anyway," Summer blurted, "I'm sorry for interrupting. What's your idea?"

"Oh, we are back to my idea now?" He put a finger up to his head and roamed his eyes around in wonderment. "Maybe I forgot the special treat I had planned for you by now," Jamie joked. Summer snatched a pillow off the bed and tossed it at his head. "Maybe that will bring your memory back," she said in laughter. Summer did laugh too. "Okay," Jamie said as he snapped himself upright. "I think we should celebrate Thanksgiving tonight in an untraditional way by finding a park and taking a picnic lunch." Jamie paused and waited to hear the squeal of excitement from his wife. A squeal he did get but not the one he was expecting. "Are you crazy?! It's freezing outside at night," Summer squealed back at him. "We have had plenty of great times in the cold. Don't bail on me now," he begged her. "Say yes and I will get on the phone and find the best park in this town," Jamie said. Summer felt his excitement and gained some of her own, so she did say yes. "Great," he yelled as he ran to the phone. "It will be a real winter adventure! Think of it as a camping trip," he told her as he picked the phone up and dialed for the hotel operator.

The operator told Jamie all about a place called Borghese Gradena. Jamie in turn told Summer. They finished packing and cleaning around 4:30, and by 5:00 they were dressed in their warmest and headed out for the garden. When they arrived at Borghese Gradena they were very surprised of the peaceful atmosphere. The place gave an escape from the city so they could have the feel of their own hometowns. Tranquil and beautiful, just as was described in all of the brochures. "Wow, this place is huge! Kind of reminds me of the park in my hometown," Summer said as she walked near a big tree and prepared the ground for their picnic.

"Yeah, and it is also not as cold as I thought it would be today," Jamie said as he watched the sheet Summer flung into the air get caught by the wind and slowly land perfectly on the ground.

"Speak for yourself," Summer told him as she zipped her coat all the way to the top and dropped to her knees onto the neatly prepared sheet. Jamie smiled, then knelt beside her and started laying out their Thanksgiving dinner, which they had picked up from a restaurant on the way over. They ate and enjoyed. The sounds of the city were soon forgotten.

After their dinner had been eaten, the silence of the park quickly faded as some vacationing college students entered the park with a football. Still, the yells and the excitement of the guys did not ruin Summer and Jamie's good mood. All was well until the football was thrown too wide. It hit smack-dab in the middle of the tree near Jamie and Summer. The ball bounced off the tree and landed in Summer's lap, bringing her and Jamie's conversation to a complete halt. After the initial shock, Summer laughed and Jamie took the ball out of her lap. One of the guys was running over to retrieve the ball, and he was screaming out his apologies from across the field. Jamie stood with the football and yelled for the guy to stop where he was as he stood in position to throw the ball back. The guy stopped, smiled, and prepared himself for the catch. Jamie took his best stance and centered his energy, throwing the ball directly to the young man. The young man caught the ball, but he still ran over to Jamie. "Good arm, dude!" the guy said to Jamie.

"Thanks," Jamie responded with pride.

"Hey, we got room for one more guy, you wanna play?" The guy asked. Jamie was tempted, then he looked down at his shivering wife and turned down his invitation. "Naw, thanks for the invite, but it's time for us to be getting out of this cold," Jamie said. Jamie turned back to Summer and began packing their things so that they could get back to the hotel.

The next day, the couple was getting excited about moving on to their next adventure. The transition from Rome to London was a smooth one. When they arrived, they took notice that the city had just as much grace and elegance as Rome. Crowne Plaza Hotel of London St. James was where the couple had chosen to spend the month of

December. At 39 degrees, the air was crisp and fresh as Summer and Jamie walked outside of the hotel. They admired the hotel's award-winning courtyard garden as they held hands. The couple found themselves drifting from the hotel and venturing out further into the streets of London. Breathing in the fresh cool air, they walked and they talked as they enjoyed every sight they saw.

"The atmosphere! The people! It's all so different here than the small town I was raised in. I never really noticed the town was small," Summer rambled on. "Visitors would always come passing through the town and they would say, 'Soooo, this is little Saratoga. Nice little town y'all got here,' they would say, not knowing they had already offended me with the 'little' remark. I would just smile and say 'why thank you,' then walk away 'cause after all, they might think our town is little, but at least they would leave knowing that Saratoga was the friendliest little town they ever did pass through and who knows, maybe one day they might come and retire."

Jamie could listen to Summer ramble on about anything all day, just to see the gleam of innocence in her eyes and the faraway look she had when she ventured off into her own mind. His favorite part about all of her stories was definitely her smile while she told them.

"The people?" Jamie questioned. "You think the people are different here too? How so?"

"Yes! Definitely! The people are way different here. Can't you tell?" she asked him.

"Uhmmm." Jamie held that tone while glancing around at the people walking the streets. "Uhm, no not really, they all seem like they put their pants on one leg at a time like the rest of us."

Summer chimed in with, "Yeah, but they slip their legs through much nicer clothes. Look at that guy," she said as she pointed to a man trying to hail a cab on the corner.

"What about him?" replied Jamie.

"To look at him answers that question, don't it?! He is dressed in an extra fine black suit with eight buttons going down the middle. And it fits him so firmly, yet comfortable looking. I bet it was tailor-made just for him. London is so full of culture, and there are so many things to do here. I wish I lived in London, but I bet they only let the beautiful live here."

Jamie stopped walking. He was still holding Summer's hand, so she came to a halt as well. Then she turned towards Jamie and asked him what was wrong. He put his hand on her left cheek and held it there ever so slightly, with the gentlest touch, and told her, "You could be the queen of London, if there be such a thing, because her beauty topped all of the lovely ladies on the street." Summer stood there in her jeans and sneakers as ladies in dresses and high-heeled boots clicked past her, but with all the glamour that surrounded her, when she looked into the eyes of a man that truly loved her and showed her all the respect in the world, then she knew. "Yes, she was the queen of the ball." After a long walk in the city, they took a cab back to the hotel. They ordered room service and enjoyed the rest of the night inside. "I enjoyed being out and about today. It was way better than what I do at home on my day off…sit around watching TV…might go out to see a movie…but then how can you really say you are going out to watch a movie? With a movie you are still on the inside! Sitting in a cramped little room. The only difference in watching a movie in the theater is the big screen and all the strangers. You can't even comment on the movie out loud. Today we walked!"

"You can walk at home," Jamie told her. Summer gave him a quick evil glance. "Yeah, but never will I see a view like the one here, and even the cold air seems different. I enjoyed it. I felt like the crisp chilled air was renewing my soul!" Summer told Jamie with extreme joy and excitement.

"Well, I am glad to hear that the cold didn't bother you, because I got a lot more cold days and nights planned for you! There's plenty of time to make the most of outdoors in London. I have a great surprise for you. I ordered us a couple of tickets for 'Around Town Ice-Skating' at the Tower of London ice-skating rink. Summer let out a sharp scream as she bounced on her knees on top of the bed. Jamie smirked. "Yep, those skating lessons are not gonna go to waste." While Summer was still screaming, Jamie threw in, "Well it's two weeks from now, but there are plenty of other skating activities on ice that we can attend to test our skills before we step out there with the pros! Even some ice-skating at night. I checked into it. I knew you would love it." Most of Summer's years she hated ice-skating, but since Jamie taught her the ropes, she was ready for the challenge.

"Let's get some rest, because tomorrow night we skate on ice."

The sun rose and so did Summer. Her bright hazel eyes popped open wide as she lay. She desired the night to come with haste before the sun even had a chance to take its proper place in the sky. Glancing to her left, she saw Jamie lying beside her sound asleep. She wanted to wake him and discuss the events for the night, but not wanting to seem like a kid on Christmas Eve, she continued to lie there in silence watching him sleep. Ten minutes passed and it seemed like an hour to Summer, so she decided it was time Jamie began his day. Summer coughed and quickly glanced over at Jamie, who had not budged an inch. So she decided to clear her throat a little louder. She just knew that would do the job, but to her amazement she got no results. Still he lay sound asleep. Well that's it, she thought as she jerked herself straight up in the bed. Repeatedly she coughed and gagged in a panic. This alarmed Jamie. He woke right away asking her what was wrong. With her hand to her mouth and in between her forcing air out of her lungs, she said to him in a very strained voice, "Just got strangled, that's all. Went down the wrong pipe." Jamie patted her on the back in an attempt to comfort her, which seemed to work well because in a matter of seconds her voice cleared. She stopped coughing and aimed all of her attention on talking to Jamie about their plans for the night. They spent most of their morning just lying in bed talking, planning, laughing, and cuddling. It was noon before they decided to get up and go find some lunch…well more like brunch since they had skipped breakfast. They found a nice restaurant around town, tucked away in a little corner kind of resembling the antique shop where Summer worked, except it had food inside instead of silk. The place served homemade cooking and was owned by an older couple who actually ran the restaurant. Betty and Bob were their names, and they just fell in love with Jamie and Summer when they met them. Betty greeted all of their guests when they entered to give them that down-home feeling. When Jamie and Summer came through the door, Betty leaned over to Bob and said, "Now those two are truly in love, I can see it in their body posture." Bob said, "Bad posture! Just 'cause they lean close to one another, doesn't mean they are in love, Betty. Lust can have that same appearance." "Oh no!" Betty responded in her best whispering voice, which wasn't very good for her or Bob since Summer and Jamie heard everything they were saying. But it didn't bother them a bit. They smiled, took each other's hand, and walked to their table; and this began a beautiful relationship between Summer, Jamie, Bob, and Betty. Betty even sent over free dessert after their brunch was over……cheesecake!! Cheesecake was her and Bob's favorite dessert, so she thought. In reality, Bob started eating cheesecake when he first met Betty because he knew she liked it and he wanted to start some common interest between the two of them. Since then, now thirty years later, he was still choking down cheesecake for dessert with a smile on his face. Betty thought since cheesecake sweetened up her love life, then maybe it would do the same for Jamie and Summer. Plus, she was hoping dessert would make them stay a little longer so she could watch them from a distance and rekindle some of that new love aroma that was floating all around the two of them. Betty sent a waitress over to give the cheesecake as she watched. It did put a smile on their faces when free cheesecake was slid on their table. Betty stood with one hand on her hip watching them with a gleam of pride in her eyes. In her mind, she had just put the final drop of glue that sealed their relationship for life. As Jamie and Summer looked at the waitress with an expression of joy and thanks, Betty looked at them with pride. Bob too had his sight on Betty. He stood head held high, staring at her, knowing exactly what she was thinking; and he had his own thoughts of pride. Proud to have a woman like Betty, whose mind wandered with thoughts like no other, with a heart of gold and the ability to see a big positive future in things that most people found bleak and turned away from.

After a great meal Summer and Jamie went back to the hotel to get rested up for the night. The time finally came for the night of the ice. Summer and Jamie were dressed in jeans, sweaters, and boots. All dressed and warm, they went out to the front of the hotel where the cab Jamie called was waiting. Summer was skipping to the cab, like an excited second-grader hyped up on sugar. Her skipping got a little off-balanced and she tripped off the curb and fell straight on her butt. Jamie rushed to her side from the other side of the cab; to his surprise, she was just sitting there flat on her butt on the side of the curb laughing. Jamie shook his head as he reached his hand out to her, all along thinking she is silly, yet loveable. When they finally made it in the cab, the ride was short. The skating rink was not too far from the hotel. They entered the building and were surprised to see so many skaters out at night. The place was much smaller than the Tower Skating Rink would be, but still nice and great for practice, they both thought. Jamie and Summer skated for hours as if they were in a marathon. No rest breaks for four hours straight, but they were just fine. They wanted to be at their best when they went to the Tower Skating Rink, where plenty of celebrities skated. They had not practiced in a while seeing how all the wedding had put skating to a halt. They skated until the lights dimmed and the announcer came over the intercom, stating that in fifteen minutes it would be midnight, and they all knew what that meant:

closing time. Since they'd found out that the skating rink was not far from the hotel, they decided to walk back. They laughed and played as they walked the streets of London stumbling into one another with big smiles on their faces, as if they were drunk from skating around in circles for hours. The couple were enjoying being with each other, with their natural high off life, and were glad it was all they needed to stay afloat. When they got back to the hotel they were so exhausted, they took off their shoes, laid across the bed together, and fell asleep fully dressed. Summer woke up the next morning with the thought that there were only ten more days before she and Jamie would skate with the celebrities at the Tower of London at their special event night. Those ten days seemed long for Summer, but she still enjoyed every minute of it. The anticipation for excitement only heightened the everyday joys she was already receiving by just being in London.

All prepared and suited up with new outfits for the night, Jamie and Summer pulled up in a cab right in front of the Tower of London. The beauty of the night blended with the glowing bright light that surrounded the tower. The sight really intrigued Jamie and Summer. There were many people outside skating with their cold noses and numb fingertips that skated the night away. The night was more than enjoyable for Summer and Jamie. Summer joined a skating dance competition and won the crowd over as she did spins in the air, skating fearlessly to the upbeat of the music that filled the night air. The cool breeze whisking through her body as she traveled on the ice mixed with the beat from the music pulsating through her body. The sound of the crowd was egging her on; it gave Summer a rush like she had never experienced. The night at London Tower Skating Rink was everything they had ever imagined and more. There were not as many celebrities there as the advertisement would have them believe, but Summer did spot a singer and an actor who was more than willing to give her an autograph.

Their last week in London had finally arrived, and Jamie knew this week would be very special because it would be Christmastime in London. Christmas was Summer's favorite time of the year, so Jamie just knew that celebrating Christmas for the first time as husband and wife in London was a fantastic idea.

It was Christmas Eve morning, and Jamie woke up really early to go shopping. He left a note on his pillow beside Summer to let her know that he would be out for the morning. All along he was thinking he had a good four hours of shopping he could do and get back even before she woke up. Jamie went to many clothing stores in London, and when he saw the prices he was very glad he had prepared for the Christmas shopping trip in his budget period. He did not want to get her gifts in advance, knowing that they would be out of town during Christmastime. He also didn't like the idea of purchasing her gift before leaving home and packing it in the luggage; he figured it would be damaged, lost, or she would see it, like he had seen his gift that Summer had been hiding in her luggage since they'd left home, but he would never tell her he saw it. He wouldn't want to upset her. Plus Jamie was planning on purchasing so many items he would have needed an extra suitcase just for her Christmas presents. He found a beautiful leather coat that he figured would look nice on her. Black leather that had a cute little dip at the hip, which Jamie thoroughly admired as the saleslady, who was about Summer's size, tried it on to give Jamie a visual of how it fit to a body. When the saleslady twirled around to the back, the coat was as good as sold. Jamie figured if the coat looked that good on the saleslady, his Summer could definitely rock it.

Off to the next store, Jamie saw a fitted dress fitted perfectly to a mannequin in the window. This demonstration drew him in immediately. As he entered the doors he was greeted by four anxious saleswomen who had spotted him staring at the dress. They admired his looks very much and hoped that he would come inside so they could look further. He walked through the door, and simultaneously he heard the four ladies ask if they could help him. He stood as two ladies stood to the left of him and two more to the right. He smiled looking straight ahead, not knowing which direction to turn. He said, "Yes, I would like to purchase in the window." The ladies bickered with one another to see who would help him. Other customers in the store turned their nose up to the situation they were witnessing because they did not recall getting the same service. The manager noticed the situation, and he went to appoint one of the ladies to assist Jamie and showed the others in the direction of the other guests lurking the store. The manager was glad that he was a man. Even he had noticed Jamie was quite handsome, and if he had been a woman all order in the store would have been lost. Jamie purchased the dress along with a few other items and even had it gift wrapped while he was there.

He made it back to the hotel and entered quietly. His wife was still asleep just like he'd hoped. He set up a small

Christmas tree, which he had purchased from the girt store in the hotel. He surrounded the tree with Summer's gift and removed the letter he left for Summer and laid back beside her. Tired from his journey, he fell asleep. As REM sleep took over Jamie's mind Summer soon woke up. She noticed Jamie lying beside her fully dressed and she knew something was up. She got off the bed slowly so as not to wake him. Quietly she placed her bunny sleepers (which were really shaped like a bunny, ears in front, fluffy tail on the heel) on her feet, practically tip-toeing to the other room. With one glance at the tree surrounded by gifts, all was silence. She looked at the tree and her heart was filled with different emotions.

Jamie woke up and rose from his bed. Summer was no longer beside him and this excited him. This meant she had seen the presentation that he'd laid out for her. He tip-toed to the door, and Jamie peeped at Summer from around the corner without her knowledge. He saw the gleam of excitement and joy in her eyes as she gazed upon the gifts he'd left for her. This view alone brought him all he needed for Christmas. Still staring at her he noticed the smile leave her face and the light dim from her eyes. Her joy had turned into sadness. What was wrong? he thought. She can't hate the gifts already, for she never opened them. The wrapping? he questioned in his head. Does she hate the wrapping paper on the gifts? The paper was in blue, her favorite color, so no, that couldn't be it either. He decided he was done standing in the shadows wondering. He moved himself from the corner quietly and gently he came up behind her, putting his hand on her shoulder. Slightly startled, she turned her head quickly towards him. She put a quick smirk on her face so as not to disappoint him. Even though her lips were formulated to a smile, the light just did not glisten in her eyes. Jamie took the comedian approach on the situation and said while smiling, "You can't hate the gifts already, you haven't even seen them yet." She turned to face him and told him that she already thought all the gifts were great because they came from him. "Well what is wrong?" he asked. Summer's eyes dropped to the ground before responding as if she had a bit of shame for what she was about to say. "I have never spent a holiday away from my family," she said. As soon as the words left her mouth, Jamie was mad at himself for not thinking that maybe she would not want to be with all of her family for Christmas. After all, it was his idea to extend the honeymoon to experience the holidays out of state. Christmas was pretty much ruined because Summer would tear up at just the sight of anything holiday like. She saw a commercial with a family gathered around a living room together eating homemade cookies and drinking milk. She started crying immediately. Jamie sat in a corner quietly in amazement, not knowing what to say. Soon the holiday was over and a new day came. It was like someone had put Summer in a time machine and took her from the bad times to the good times. Yesterday was gone and she was on to the new with a smile on her face and the light back in her eyes. From London to Paris, Summer and Jamie traveled to their final honeymoon destination in style. They flew first-class and being this was Summer's third flight in two months, she was now a pro and feeling calm and collected. After they landed in Paris, Jamie took his wife by the hand as they walked through the airport and he told her that he had saved the best for last. She smiled as she heard him, while still holding his hand and eyes traveled from corner to corner taking in her surroundings. Jamie stopped walking and this caused Summer to draw all of her attention to him. She turned and looked at him with an expression of confusion on her face. Looking her directly in her eyes and still holding her hand with his left hand, he took his other hand and reached into his pocket, pulling out an envelope. He handed it to her. She looked at it. As soon as she saw her name on the envelope, she snatched her hand away from Jamie and immediately began ripping the envelope apart. Jamie barely got the word "careful" out of his mouth when hundreds of dollars fell from the badly torn envelope onto the floor. They both dropped to their knees quickly while glancing around them at all of the strangers gasping in their direction. Summer was so excited that she was grabbing cash from every direction while repeatedly saying, "Oh my gosh, oh my gosh!" She got so excited after she stuffed the money she had collected in her pocket that she immediately snatched the cash that Jamie held in his hands. She had a straight face while doing this, which caused Jamie to break out in laughter. The couple definitely did not go unnoticed in the lobby of the city's airport. A man came and told them their luggage was being placed in the cab courtesy of the airport. Jamie was still laughing, and Summer kneeled towards the floor with her hand over her mouth while scooting out of the airport quietly. While they were riding to the hotel where they would be staying, Summer finally asked what the package was for. He told her it was for her to have a grand shopping trip in Paris! Mouth gasping wide with a screeching sound protruding the air, Summer fell on Jamie's shoulder. She was happy, he was happy. They arrived at the hotel and this began their trip in Paris. This hotel was just as delightful as the last two, the couple thought. It was a late flight so they retired for the night with plans to shop all morning. Jamie woke before Summer and snuck out quietly. He went downstairs to the lobby area, where there was a little gift shop and a café. He entered the gift shop and purchased a single rose along with a small white teddy bear. He was only going to buy the rose, but the teddy bear really got his attention because he had never seen one with blue eyes. He stared at him a second all blank faced, then he snapped out of it, looked at the cashier, and said, "Please charge it to my account." From there, he walked across the hall to the café and purchased a bowl of soup with some toast on the side and a small carton of orange juice. The cashier looked at his order and thought it to be rather weird for 8 am. He sat in the lobby until he was called to get his food. He grabbed the bag and said, "Please charge it to my room." He started walking away when he remembered he'd left his bag from the gift store in the chair he was sitting on. The young lady at the counter watched him as he retraced his steps. He grabbed the bag and began his walk toward the elevator again. A little bit closer to the exit this time, but again he turned. The lady was still watching him; this time he came back to her and asked if he could get two packs of grape jelly. "Sure," she said as she turned to retrieve them. She handed them to him and placed them in his bag and again he was on his way. She continued to watch him and was so proud when he rounded the corner towards the elevator. He had made it this time. He got back to the room and Summer was sound asleep just like he'd hoped. He placed his items down on the table with every attempt at being quiet. His teddy bear had bumped into the pencil that lay on the table next to a notepad, courtesy of the hotel, and it began to roll. Jamie, in a slight panic, scooted to the floor quickly and caught it just as it rolled to the edge of the table. He gathered his composure and placed the soup, orange juice, and teddy bear on the little serving tray. He placed it in the bed beside Summer and then walked around and kissed her on the cheek. She woke up, saw Jamie, and smiled with a hazy look on her face. She turned to her right and saw the tray of food and squealed with delight. "Aww, it's soup for breakfast," she said. "You knew I hated eggs; this marriage truly is starting off right!"

The couple spent their first week shopping at all of the fine stores. Summer was in charge! Jamie followed her all around Paris, but he didn't mind because he said this gave him a chance to see his lady at her finest. Summer tried on expensive dresses that she knew she could not afford, just so she could model Paris's finest for Jamie. It was her own personal modeling session, because Jamie even bought a camera and snapped many pictures of Summer modeling the dresses.

Their second week in Paris, they traveled around the city viewing all the sites that they could take in. They saw beautiful sites that they considered breathtaking (of course the Eiffel Tower) that week. The third week, they chose to relax with no plans in particular. The last night they spent in Paris, Jamie wanted to make memorable. He had planned a night that Summer would not soon forget. He had planned a horse and carriage ride at night in Paris downtown. The streets were romantically lit up, especially Concorde Square. As Summer rode on the carriage beside Jamie, she thought she was a real princess. He had her dress in a ballroom type of dress that fluffed out at the end. He even placed a tiara on her head, so that she could pretend it was a crown. At the end of a pleasantly quiet ride, Jamie stepped down and stood back and looked at Summer, who held all of the elegance of a real princess. After gazing upon her for awhile, he held his hand out for her, and just as she leaned over to take his hand, the horse got out of control and took off down the street. The princess-like elegance Summer held quickly turned into a not so graceful look of horror. She started screaming, and the man who was controlling the carriage ride was begging her to stop. He said it was only making the horse more hysterical. He finally got him under control, and Summer got down with her hair all frizzed and a piece of her dress torn from snatching against the carriage. Jamie ran to her side and asked was she okay. She really never answered him; she just gave him a look that told him all he needed to know. The coach driver apologized repeatedly. "Crazy horse got spooked by a silly little mouse, that's all!" Summer held Jamie tightly as the man apologized. Jamie told the coach driver everything was fine and reached in his pocket as Summer was still clenched to his body and pulled out some money to tip the guy. Then they walked off together and got in the cab that was waiting for them up the street. Jamie had already paid him in advance to wait until the ride was over. By the time they arrived back at the hotel, Summer had calmed down and she was smiling with the thoughts of the pleasant part of the ride.

They returned to their hotel, "Paris Hotel de Ville," which was so beautiful at night to them, they sat outside for awhile admiring the lights and how the hotel overlooked a beautiful pond. The next morning, while packing their bags as they began preparation for their twenty hour flight, they realized they no longer had enough luggage to carry all of their items and clothing. Jamie rushed to the store, where he bought a couple more luggage bags, while Summer stayed at the hotel room throwing everything they owned on top of the bed. When Jamie returned, the clutter was unbearable to him, so he immediately began packing the clothes away. The two of them questioned each other about why they hadn't packed the night before as they rushed out of the hotel. By the time they got to the airport, people were already boarding the plane. They had made it right on time. Exhausted, the two of them slept on and off for most of their flight, when the plane finally landed near their hometown. They stepped off slowly and quietly with different thoughts passing through their heads, random thoughts from both. Okay, now what? Man I wish we were back in Europe. So, real marriage life begins. Snapping out of their random thoughts as they saw a crowd of friends and family standing at the gate holding up signs with bold words on saying "Welcome Home!", they excitedly greeted their friends and family. They were immediately embraced and swarmed with questions about the trip. Finally someone stepped in and said for everyone to back off and give Summer and Jamie a break so they could get settled in the real world of marriage. The thought kind of frightened the couple a bit, but they said, "We have been married for three months now and things are going fine, so leaving the honeymoon and going home can't be that much of a transition." When this was said out loud amongst the crowd, some of the older couples laughed and shook their heads. Their friends tried to wait around for them to leave in the cab, but they had sat around talking for an hour and the luggage had not been retrieved from the plane yet. The luggage claim was really backed up. Friends started saying their good-byes and leaving one by one, until finally it was three hours later and Jamie and Summer sat alone. Three and a half hours later, the luggage was finally retrieved and was being placed in the cab with apologies from the airport about the long wait. The ride home was quiet and strange. No talking, no snuggle; each in their own corner looking out the window wondering what's to be. The cab pulled up to Jamie's house and he got out. Summer just sat in the cab as if she were waiting on the next stop. Jamie walked around and opened the door for her. Still, Summer did not move or speak. She had an unsure look on her face mixed with a bit of sadness. Jamie stared at her for a moment, then he tilted his head down and reached his hand out for her. Slowly but surely, she moved out of the cab. Jamie and the cab driver put all of the luggage on the front porch. Summer just stood back in the yard watching. When the cab driver drove away, still she stood back away from the porch quietly. Jamie was unlocking the house and dragging luggage inside and still she didn't move. Finally placing the last piece on the inside, he turned and noticed her. "Well come on in," he said. "I don't have to invite you; you aren't a guest anymore." Summer walked toward him and onto the porch; she was still hesitant to move through the door. She had never even spent a full night at Jamie's house, and now she was to consider this her home. Jamie turned to look at the big cluster of stuff in his house. "Come on," he said, "we got to get to work organizing everything, our family and friends did just what they said they would and brought all of your things over from your apartment. They just didn't organize a thing," he said while shaking his head in amazement because the cluttered house was not his thing. Summer sighed and entered the house, and Jamie was so preoccupied with the mess that he did not take notice that she was still very sad. They spent the next month organizing and redecorating the house to suit both of them. It was not an easy task, but the work was finally done. Jamie and Summer were in the process of settling down in their new life together. Summer decided that she wanted to continue working at Slick Ladies Silk even though it was a forty-five minute commute every day. Summer's boss, who was also the owner of the store, had decided to make Summer the manager of the store. Her boss had planned on being away for the next six months with plans to do a little traveling herself, so she figured why not go for it and make her favorite employee the manager while she was away? Plus, she was hoping it would give Summer a little incentive to stay working at a place that was forty-five minutes away from her house. Summer was enjoying her new status in life: the wife of a big-time CEO in marketing and now a manager. Many of the ladies around town envied her, so they tried to find a way to make her life seem a little less perfect by approaching her with the traditional question of "When you gonna get some biscuits in that oven…the pitter patter of little feet in the house?" Summer would just smile and tell them that she and Jamie had decided to wait a while on that one so that they could situate their lives together first. Hearing this put a twinkle in their eyes and caused them to glance about at one another with an uppity look with thoughts that said "Aha!" They need to situate their lives; I knew things weren't as perfect as they seemed. As they walked away with their smirks and their heads held high, Summer stood with a confused face as they walked away from her. She thought for a moment about what she'd just said and how they must have took it. "No!" she yelled. "No problems to situate, just wanna get comfortable with each other first." The women kept walking and raised their heads even higher in the air. Summer decided to stop talking before she made things worse.

Summer was back at the store when the door opened at the antique shop; she looked up and it was Jamie. He had taken off work early and came all the way over just to take her to lunch. They ate at a little sandwich shop around the corner from Slick Ladies Silk. "Summer," Jamie called as he sat across the table from her. "I have been having something on my mind for a couple of weeks now that I want to discuss with you. I really wish I had thought of it a lot earlier, but anyway hindsight is 20/20, so let's move forward."

"What's up?" Summer interrupted.

"Well…I was thinking that it really was not fair to ask you to move into my place after we got married."

Summer spoke up. "Well there was no way that the two of us would have been comfortable in my cramped little apartment."

"Well I was thinking maybe we should have looked for a new place together that had an appeal that we both liked… plus we could have found a house halfway between both of our jobs."

"Yeah, that would have been a good idea."

Jamie said in a hesitant voice, "Well we could still do it if you would like."

Summer looked at him and smiled. "That was so sweet of you, but I'm just getting settled in and I'm not going anywhere." Summer knew that Jamie would not have been happy leaving his home, but she was delighted by the offer because it meant she had a very considerate man.

It had been six months now since they had returned from the honeymoon. Summer was sitting on the couch polishing her fingernails when Jamie came up to her with his camera phone snapping pictures. He was looking at her with that gleam of love that he held in his eyes only for her, as she sat there with a look of boredom. They had been home long enough now that they had got in a routine with everyday life, and Summer was feeling that the honeymoon was definitely over. Though none of this she said out loud as she looked up with her polish in one hand and her brush in the other while she posed for the camera with a small smirk on her face. The weeks had come and gone. The growths of the new season had begun to peek. Flowers had begun to bloom and the grass appeared a little greener to those who wandered their eyes across the fields.

The phone rang suddenly, startling Summer. "Slick Ladies Silk, this is Summer speaking, how can I help you?"

"May I speak to a manager?" a weak shrill voice creaked through the phone lines.

"Yes ma'am! You're speaking to her," Summer responded while at the same time, she was making change for a person in front of her. "Thank you!" she said as she placed the money in the frail hand of the older woman.

"Thanks for what?" the lady on the phone spoke up.

"Oh no. I'm sorry," Summer said, "I was talking to a customer."

"Oh, so I'm *not* a customer?"

"Oh no, I mean yes," Summer squeaked out while stumbling over her words trying not to offend. Clearly she spoke up now, "I am so sorry, it is just so busy in the store today." The second she said that, three more ladies entered the store. Summer, who was working alone today due to another employee calling in sick, called out, "How can I help you?!" She was very overwhelmed when the lady on the phone started saying what she needed, as well as the three young ladies walking over all talking at the same time. When Summer finally cleared things up for the day, she was exhausted. She went home and told Jamie all about her day. He suggested that she hire some extra help, because after all, they were short one person now since Summer's boss was away. Summer said, "I thought we ladies could handle things, but the store is getting a lot busier since summertime came in. I guess you are right, I will put an ad in the paper tomorrow. I will try to find someone soon." Summer did just what she said, and the next morning the first place she went was the newspaper agency. Walking out of the building to a warm, sunny summer day, she had hopes for a more relaxing new beginning at work. The day had come and gone since her ad had run in the paper. Three days had passed and not one person came to fill out an application, and the store had definitely gotten no less busy. This frustrated Summer, so she decided to post wanted signs on the doors of the store. Also, she wondered where her mind was that she had not thought of doing it before. The hour she put the sign up, she had people asking her for applications. Unfortunately, no one ever seemed to bring them back. Summer went to lunch leaving one of her employees, Joanne, in charge of the store.

When she returned she was surprised when Joanne ran up to her with a completed application in her hand. "Look, look, check it out," Joanne yelled to Summer in the finally empty store. "This person came in and did an application; he filled it out sitting right here and went ahead and turned it in."

"He?" Summer questioned, not even reaching her hand out for the application Joanne was excitedly reaching her, since it was the only one turned in. "Yes! He, but friendly," Joanne said. Summer tightly squeezed her lips and scrunched up her nose as she began to turn away from Joanne and the application. "I wanted all ladies working in a silk shop," Summer whined. "OH-kay," Joanne lingered as she turned and walked away, placing the application under the counter at the front desk.

Another week had passed and the days seemed even longer and busier. Several more people had picked up applications but in the return pile; still "the one" lay there alone. Exhausted one evening, Summer and Joanne closed up shop quietly. On the way out the door, Summer had a white towel in her hand which she had used for dusting. She sighed deeply, threw the towel behind her, and told Joanne to call the guy tomorrow and set up a time for an interview as she walked on with a feeling of defeat. Joanne, who was walking directly behind her, had a smile on her face and a feeling of accomplishment. The next morning came and Joanne bounced into work an hour early. She skipped over to the counter and snatched up the application with her left hand and reached for the phone that lay directly on top of the counter with her right. She called the applicant and set up an interview for that very same day. She wanted to set the appointment before Summer could get to work and change her mind. When Summer got to the store the first thing she said to Joanne was, "Maybe we will get some more applications by the end of the day, so we can hold off on calling that mister." Joanne listened and smiled, saying nothing. Summer recognized the face of satisfaction on Joanne. Summer, now with a stern face, took a step backwards shaking her head no while pointing one finger at Joanne. "You didn't," she said, "not already…no you didn't!" Joanne's smile spread wider as she said, "Yes ma'am, just following orders," and then she slowly backed away.

"Well what day is he coming in?" Summer yelled from across the room. Joanne backed a little closer to the storage room, then yelled back, "He will be here today at two o'clock." Joanne barely got "two o'clock" out of her mouth before Summer let a loud childish scream out and Joanne sprinted for the back room.

Soon it was time for the store to open. Summer asked Joanne if she would do the honors because she needed to go in the back and prepare for the interview, which was something she had never done (well at least not from the hiring side of the desk).

She sat in the office with a pen in her hand, and a blank sheet of paper lay on top of the solid red oak desk. Summer began tapping the red oak with a steady rhythm in hopes that a thought would come to her head telling what kind of interview question she should ask. The tapping did not work at all. Still her mind was blank on the subject, and so was the piece of paper that lay on the desk. A ringing phone snapped her out of her daze. She answered it and it was her husband. As soon as she heard Jamie's voice, she sharply said, "This is perfect!" in his ear. "Oh-kay," Jamie said, "I'm glad you think I'm perfect; you aren't so bad yourself."

"No, silly, I have an interview scheduled for today that I just found out about this morning and my mind is really blank for questions. I've never done nothing like this, but you being CEO in your own marketing agency, I bet you could give me some tips!"

"Oh well, yes ma'am," Jamie quickly responded. "In fact, give me your fax number. I have a set of questions I use as a guideline for what I want to know. You just have to tweak a few words and make it apply to silk, but they are pretty basic questions though; it should help. In addition to the questions, keep your eyes open for mood swings, gang tattoos, and just anything weird when you are talking to her."

Summer said "thank you" while thinking at the same time Jamie just called the applicant a "her." Summer wondered if she should correct him and let him know it was a man. The thought quickly passed; she decided against a correction and the next thing out of her mouth was her fax number.

"Okay thanks, sweetie," Jamie said. "I will fax it to you now. I hope it helps, don't be nervous when talking to her because you want to start the relationship off with you in charge. Don't let her see an opening to walk all over you, but don't be mean or rude either…well keep it all in mind. Oh, and have fun," Jamie said with a laugh just before he hung up the phone.

The fax shortly came and Summer laid it on top of her blank piece of paper with an even blanker expression than before. Summer sat trying to comprehend all that Jamie had said. Somehow hearing the words "don't be nervous" really enhanced the feeling. Summer was deep in thought when a knock at the office door allowed her mind to let go and relax a little as she redirected her mind to think of a task a lot more simple, like forcing her lips to push out the words "come in." It was Joanne telling Summer it was almost two o'clock, and Summer should take lunch first so she could relax a bit for her two o'clock interview. Summer thought that was a good idea. She got up from the desk and thanked Joanne as she passed by her and headed for the door. Already full from her own nerves, Summer decided she couldn't eat, but still a break was needed, so she headed for the park. She arrived and took a blanket out of her trunk and laid it under the old apple tree and just lay there trying to relax as she often did as a teenager. As she lay there with her eyes closed, she thought about how the warm air comforted her, and the big tree shaded her eyes from the sun's direct contact; and how the chirping birds flowed freely around her. The atmosphere had relaxed her but before she knew it, her lunch hour was almost up and she found herself dragging back to her car with the tail of her blanket trailing behind her. When she entered the store, Joanne popped up with her keys in her hands. "I hope you had a good lunch," she said as she walked past her. "I gotta hurry so I can be back before the interview starts; I can cover the front desk so you won't be disturbed." That Joanne; always thinking, Summer thought as she walked towards a customer to ask if she could help her pick out some silk.

Thirty minutes later Joanne came back to Slick Ladies Silk with a fast-food bag in her hand. Summer approached her. "You're back early." "Yep! I didn't want to miss our visitor. Besides, it looks more professional if you are already in your office when he arrives. I will bring him to you."

"Uhm…interesting," Summer said with a nodding head.

"Yep, girl, you have got to get into the mind of management," Joanne replied with laughter. Summer turned and walked to her office. Joanne waited at the front with anticipation of their visitor. Summer sat in her office for a while reviewing the interview questions. She was much calmer than before. One split-second caused a thought to rush to Summer's head, taking away the calmness immediately. All of this time she'd never reviewed the application. She had been too busy running from it, because she didn't want to hire a man. She panicked; she jumped out of her chair and was heading for the door when she tripped, falling and catching herself with her hands just before her face hit the floor. She was on her hands and knees as she looked around to see what she'd tripped over. Nothing, it seemed. She stood, dusted herself off, and headed for the door again.

"Joanne, let me see that application," Summer called out.

"Okay, as soon as I get off the phone I will grab it for ya. These inventory people have got me on hold again," Joanne screeched.

"Okay, I will wait." Summer went back to her office. Joanne waited a minute more for inventory to come back to the phone. When she found herself still listening to the phone music, she hung up and went to find where she had put the application. It was no longer under the counter. She thought for a second about where she might have placed it. She walked to the storage room and it was there, lying on top of a box of silk scarves. She grabbed it and dusted some crumbs off of it that had come off her sandwich earlier. She rushed it to Summer; she walked into the office with not even a tap on the door. She placed it on Summer's desk with excitement, stating, "Here you are!" Joanne stood over her as Summer gazed at the application with amazement.

"What's up?" Joanne asked.

"That name," Summer responded. "It seemed way too familiar."

"What? Jason Camridge?" Joanne asked as she called out the name on the application.

"Jason Camridge," Summer said slowly. "Yes…in fact that name is more than familiar. If this is the same guy, I went to high school with him; I met him as a freshman. Yep, ninth grade, but it can't be him because, just before we all started our senior year, his dad got a job in New York and took Jason. They moved that summer just before twelfth grade started."

"Interesting," Joanne said, "well, good then, you already know him." The door opened, making a chiming sound. "Well that must be him," Joanne said with a smile. "Wait here and I will bring him to you." Joanne walked off before Summer could tell her what else made the name "Jason Camridge" so special. Camridge was Summer's first boyfriend, and when he moved away, she never got the opportunity to say good-bye, which made getting over him extremely hard. Summer and Jason dated from ninth grade all the way through the eleventh grade, only separating because of the forced move made by his father to better his career.

A knock at the office door. Summer heard it. She sat, her breathing got deeper, and her eyes wider. The knock sounded again and her heartbeat bounced a little faster. She looked down at her chest to see if her shirt was moving since the pounding of her heart was so intense. Finally, she took a deep breath, and as she let it out she said, "Come in." Oh no, she thought, there is no turning back now. All was silent for just one second and then the door began to creep open. The door swung open, and Summer stood to her feet. She and Jason were face to face—again. Joanne immediately started with the introductions. If she had taken the time to look at the expressions on Summer and Jason's faces, she would have known there was no introduction necessary. The two stood in silence, staring at each other as Joanne rambled on with excitement in hopes that they were about to get some help in the store. Eventually, she stopped talking, noticing Summer and Jason had not mumbled a word to each other. She took it that they were both nervous, so she backed out of the room quietly, gently closing the door behind her. Summer was at a loss for words; still she stood there in silence and a blank look rested on her face. As he heard the door click closed, Jason emerged from his initial shock of seeing Summer again for the first time in many years. He began pacing from side to side, with his eyes captured on Summer much like a lion does its prey. "What?" Summer said with a sideways smile and one raised eye. Though only hearing one word, the sound of her voice enhanced Jason's emotion of joy a hundredfold. He paced on in front of her desk, but never taking his eyes off of her. He began biting the bottom of his lips, which showed off his perfectly white teeth. They went very well with his smooth tanned skin. As he bit his bottom lip, it also brought attention to his baby-fine mustache that could have easily belonged to a sixteen-year-old boy. The texture of it was perfectly smooth and soft. His hair was cut low with waves all in it, showing off the naturally fine texture. Jason was born in Hawaii and that was how most women explained his good looks. Though Summer was flattered by all of the pacing, smiling, and biting that was aimed directly at her, she figured she had better stop this quickly. She had glanced at his left hand and there was no ring on his finger. "Where are my manners?" Summer said in an attempt to stop the weirdness. "Please sit down." Jason did sit down, but still he stared at her. "So how have you been? It's been like forever since I've seen you," Summer said.

"Well, I have got to say"—as he looked her up and down while she was still standing—"I have definitely not been as fine as you."

"Wow…..well…...oh-kay. We better get started with this interview." Summer started with some basic interview questions, but she honestly could not focus on the answers he was giving. He noticed she was kind of out of it, and hoped that this did not mean he was not going to get the job. Now more than ever, he really wanted to work at Slick Ladies Silk. He remembered Summer's soft spot for those in need. So he stopped, got very serious, and said, "Can I be honest with you? I had a great job, making big money; but I lost it about five months ago and unemployment just ain't cutting it. I've been putting in apps everywhere with no bites. I already had to move to a cheaper, smaller house. Pretty soon my unemployment is going to run out and I might lose the little house too. I don't want to move back with my dad in New York. I'm a grown man now in my thirties. He would be so disappointed in me." Jason saw the emotions flicker in Summer's eyes and he knew he had got her. All of Summer's thoughts and good judgment were contrary to the next words out of her mouth.

"Okay. You are hired, you can start tomorrow."

Jason stood, quickly placing that gorgeous smile back on his face. "Thank you," he said as he reached out to shake her hand. As he stood there shaking her hand, he thought about his original purpose for applying at Slick Ladies Silk, which was to meet women. Now it was all to conquer the ONE woman who got away.

Summer went home and told Jamie all about her new hire. He was a little shocked that it was a man, but still he had no qualms about it because he completely trusted his wife. If she was happy with her new hire, then so was he. Summer got up an hour earlier than normal. She washed herself in the shower ten minutes longer and afterwards, she rubbed baby oil all over her body. This gave her that soft, fresh womanly fragrance that she was going for. She dressed herself in a pair of flirty-fitting blue jeans and a black top that revealed just a little more of the top of her cleavage than she normally showed. She added just a little more baby oil, causing the skin to look even more radiant. She topped the outfit off by placing some black four-inch heels on her feet when normally she would complain about even wearing two inch heels. When Jamie saw her walk out of the bathroom, his eyes blared wide to take it all in and his nose could not help but to take in the soft flowery fragrance protruding off her body from the baby oil. The first words out of his mouth were, "Are WE taking the day off?!"

"No!" she quickly responded. "I'm already dressed for work. What are you talking about?!"

"Oh. Okay. I just thought you were dressed for a date or something and wanted me to take the day off to take you out."

"No," she said in a quieter tone and slight look of shame on her face. She said nothing else. She walked down the stairs, took her keys off the hook, and let herself out of the house quietly. The door closed with only a faint click behind her. Summer arrived at work a little earlier than normal, so she expected to see no one there. To her surprise, she pulled up and Jason was standing at the front door pacing from side to side. She stumbled out of her car, rushing up to the front door. She scrambled for the correct key as she stood close to the doorknob and was asking him what he was doing there two hours early. "Good employees are always early," he said as he stood back admiring her completely while she faced the door scrambling for the key. He noticed her still scrambling for the key, so he stepped closer in to her, now standing directly behind her back. Summer felt his presence and froze there for a moment, no longer fumbling for the keys at all. He reached out his hand, gently glancing it across her hand as he took the keys from her slowly. "Looks like you're a little nervous this morning. Please allow me," he said in a deep soothing voice that caused Summer to take a deep relaxing breath that she exhaled in ease as her hand muscles loosened, allowing Jason to take the keys easily. Jason did not know which key was the store key, but he chose one and placed it in with ease; and it was a perfect fit. He backed up and allowed Summer to enter the store first. She walked across the room not saying a word. Jason stood at the door. He said something in a hushed voice that she could not hear. "Huh?" she said as she stepped in towards him a little closer. He did repeat himself, but this time his voice seemed even softer. "Huh?!?" she said again; "What are you saying?" she said as she stepped in now even closer. Now she stood directly in front of him and he said nothing, only smiled. His hushed voice had worked. He'd used it with the sole purpose to draw her in closer to him. She looked confused as she saw the smile on his face and heard the silence in the room. Weren't you trying to say something? she thought to herself. She moved one leg backwards in an attempt to move away since he was not talking, but just at that moment he stepped in closer. He leaned towards her left shoulder and began whispering in her ear. He was saying to her, "thank you for giving me this job position," but he might as well have been telling her how beautiful he thought she was and how sweet he thought she smelled, because that was what he wanted to say, and when she felt his warm breath projecting towards her neck, that was not only what he wanted to say but it was also what she wanted to hear. The store phone rang and Summer backed away quickly, walking towards the phone with a fast pace while saying sharply, "Yeah, sure, you're welcome. We all need work." She was flustered and practically panting for air when she answered the phone. It was Joanne who was calling in sick, and was so glad to be able to with the new help and all. When Joanne heard the tone of Summer's voice, she thought she might have been sick as well. Summer assured her that she was feeling just fine. Soon it was time for the store to open and the day went on quite busily. Jason did very well for his first day. He jumped right in with helping to get sales, and he was surprisingly very knowledgeable about the silk. For once, Summer was glad for such a busy day—that way she could avoid talking to Jason. She definitely did not mind talking to him, but even though the conversation was simple, she still felt guilty for some unexplained reason. With the fast-paced work, time went by quickly. It was lunchtime and the place had cleared out. Summer told Jason he could leave for his lunch, and Jason asked her to join him. She said no, she didn't think it was a good idea because her husband might not like it.

"Ohhhh, husband, huh. So you got married on me?"

"Yep! Husband!"

"Well I'm not asking for your hand in marriage. I just want to eat lunch at the same place and time with you. You do eat, right? I eat, you eat, so we should do it together." Again Summer said "no" while walking away. Besides, someone needed to cover the store.

"I will stay here until you get back and then I will go."

"Well okay, but give me a call if you change your mind."

As he walked out the door, he told her he would be glad to come back for her. As the door closed shut, Summer stood there staring towards it imagining if she had walked out of the door with him. Again a ringing phone jerked her from her daze and she walked off towards it. When the day finally ended, Summer was happy. It was nice talking with Jason again. In the past, when they were dating, she spoke with him every day and he was her comfort. She would talk to him during her forty-five minute ride home. Summer talked to Suzi from her cell phone and told her all about her day and her new employee, Jason. Suzi remembered him well. Secretly she was always jealous of him and Summer's relationship. Not because she wanted Jason but simply because she hated how much time they spent together. It took away from the time she wanted to spend with Summer; after all, they were "best" friends. Summer pulled into the driveway to her and Jamie's home. Jamie heard her pull up outside and he ran out making a skip across the steps with a loving smile on his face. He lifted the door handle to the car and pulled it open before she had a chance. With a sharp-pitched tone and quickened speech he said, "What's up, baby love, good to see you. How was your day?" he asked, but not giving her time to respond he reached out for her, pulling her out of the car closing the door behind her. "Hurry, come inside," he said. "I have a surprise for you." Summer entered the house cautiously and Jamie told her to close her eyes. He stepped up from behind her and placed his hands across her eyes, walking her slowly into the dining room. When he removed his hands and her sight was revealed again, she saw the dining-room table prepared to the fullest for a party of two. Lit candles decorated the center, and her favorite foods were spread across the table in no particular order. There was a plate of fried chicken wings sitting next to a plate of chocolate-covered cherries, and a plate of lasagna sitting next to a plate with a sliced-up honey bun by it. All of her favorite foods were laid out on one table—how nice, she thought; a little weird to see it all at once, but still nice. Jamie was the same sweet, silly person she'd married, and she adored him. After a wonderful night with her husband, she woke up with a renewed faith for her marriage, and she went to work with a mind to do right. To be a completely professional supervisor when it came to her relationship with Jason. Summer arrived at work before everyone, and she paced the floor speaking out loud, encouraging herself. "The past is the past," she mumbled, "the past is the past."

Joanne entered the store with a refreshed look upon her face. She spoke to Summer and asked how Jason's first day was. Summer told her that he was very handy with sales and she was very much surprised to know he knew a lot about the fabrics they sold. Jason came to work not too long after Joanne. They all worked well together and lunchtime quickly approached them. Jason went up to Summer and asked her to go to lunch with him. Before she could answer, he reminded her that her excuse for yesterday was the store needed to stay open. Today Joanne was there, and she could cover the store for them. He even said she could take the first lunch. After all that talking, he eventually stopped and said, "Well, are you going? I can pay for lunch, not a problem at all."

Summer spoke and said, "Well, really, I can afford my own lunch thank you very much."

Jason said, "Okay, you can buy my lunch. Anything you want, but does that mean you accept my lunch invite?"

"I told you, I'm married."

"Well what does that got to do with anything, again I say it's a lunch invite, not a wedding proposal."

Shortly after him saying that, Joanne came out of the back room and suggested that they went ahead to lunch. After hearing that, Jason turned from Joanne and looked directly at Summer with one eyebrow raised with the suggestion that she should take her up on the invitation. Summer's eyes rolled up a little as she began to accept defeat.

"All right, lunch it is, but I'm driving my own car. And you can follow me, 'cause we're gonna eat where Mom likes."

Jason liked the sassiness she was portraying. He grinned as he reached for his car keys from his pocket and followed her out the door with a swagger as if he were hearing music in his head that no one else could. One hour and thirty minutes later, they reentered Slick Ladies Silk with much laughter and apologies to Joanne for being late. She said "what ever" and walked out a little ill from hunger. Summer was glad she went to lunch with him. She told him she hadn't laughed that much in a long time. He was glad to hear that. He told her there was plenty more to come with a sneaky little grin on his face. They had talked about old times and brought many great memories back to Summer which she treasured all night. She went home overjoyed. Jamie didn't know what had come over her, but he enjoyed seeing her so happy and uplifted again. Summer had enjoyed the conversation they'd had so much that she went to lunch with him again the next day. Jason had been a perfect gentleman, so she did not see any harm in going to lunch with him; so she enjoyed lunch with him for the next two weeks. She even decided it was okay to ride in the same car with him. By the second week, they were carpooling. One day, he would drive; one day, she would drive. Times at work for Summer were grand, but at home, Jamie was feeling a little less comforted. Running down the stairs she yelled to him her good-byes as she hurried to work in her best attire. Jamie rushed to the top of the stairs just in time to see the door slam and vase on the stand beside it crash to the floor, leaving the broken pieces for Jamie to attempt to repair. Jamie sighed. He had hoped for at least a hug this morning before Summer ran off. He would have settled for a good-bye that wasn't fleeing down the stairs. Face to face, eye to eye like they used to do with a gentle kiss on the lips and a sweet smile which always followed.

Jamie spent the rest of his day at home, tending to housework on his day off. Constant thoughts of Summer ran through his head. He wondered what he had done to cause such a distance between the two of them. He wondered what he should do to bring Summer's mind back and focused on him again. All day, Jamie dusted and vacuumed, washed, dried, and folded clothes. After work, Summer pulled up in the yard. Jamie heard a car, so he peeped out of the wood blinds of the front window. He noticed her on her cell phone chattering away with bursting smiles every few seconds. Her hair was all fluffed out and hanging, much different from the ponytail she usually ended up with at the end of a hard workday. Normally, Jamie would have rushed to her side pulling the car door open for her before she had the chance. This time, he chose to watch her from afar and enjoy the smile on her face. All weekend at home, she barely grinned. Jamie attempted to amuse her with his jokes, but he had no luck. Going back to work Monday seemed to have brightened her spirits. Jamie figured she really enjoyed her new position as a manager. After all, this was her first opportunity to be boss. He stood there for five minutes, watching her enjoying a phone conversation. He figured she was telling Suzi all about her day and newfound adventures as management. He did eventually walk away from the window, and entered the kitchen in time to turn off the timer and stove and remove the pork chops from the oven. He placed the final seasoning on in and was very excited about Summer bringing some of her happiness and bright smiles in the house. He had time to put a pork chop and some broccoli on her plate and his and she still was not in the house. He took the extra time to pour their drinks and light a single candle in the direct center of the table. When the fire blazed, the door cracked open and he smiled with delight. "I'm in here, sweetie," he yelled out. The next sound he heard was not one that he was expecting. No "hello," no "good evening," but only the sound of high heel shoes trampling quickly up the steps. Had she not heard him call out for her? he wondered. Hum, he thought, even if she had heard, surely she smelt the aroma of fine cooking coming from the dining room. He walked up the stairs and stood at the top calling her name. Again he was left with an empty void. He walked in the bedroom and could hear Summer in the bathroom talking to someone. Still on the phone, he thought. Wow, it's not like her to talk this long to Suzi straight out of work.

"Summer!" he called out again as he stood right next to the bathroom door, this time with more strength and power behind his voice.

"Yeah!" she yelled back.

"Dinner is ready downstairs whenever you are. I will be down waiting for you…okay?" he questioned.

"Yeah sure! Be down in a minute!" she yelled back, then immediately continued talking on the phone in a muffled voice.

Jamie couldn't make out their conversation, but he did pick out that her mood while talking to him was not quite as friendly. He went down to give her some privacy. He sat at the table waiting for her so long that the candle had begun to melt down to almost nothing. He went ahead and blew it out and began eating his food. By the time he was at his last bite, he heard a voice behind him saying, "Wow! You couldn't even wait for me to eat dinner." She walked by him practically rolling her eyes. "Oh you couldn't light a candle," she bickered out loud towards him as he sat in silence. "Guess the romance has just gone straight out of this marriage," she said while dragging her chair out across the floor, making an awful noise. She flopped herself in front of the plate which her husband had prepared for her. After one bite, she slammed her fork down on the plate, yelling out as she pushed her chair backwards again, sliding it across the beautiful gray marble floor. "This food is cold!! You stayed home all day and I can't get a hot plate!" She stood leaning on the table looking down on him as he sat looking humble and defeated in silence. She rambled on at him and he never said a word. "…and who gets Mondays off at work anyway. Mr. Big C-E-O does, that's who!!" She started storming off, mumbling, "…so I work hard all day and I can't even get a hot plate of food." The dining-room door swung closed as she whisked by them. Jamie allowed the top half of his body to drop, slamming his head on the table. He sat with his forehead glued to the table face down wondering about…he wasn't sure, but he definitely knew that there was something to wonder about. He stayed at the table for a while. Then he decided to go upstairs and talk with his wife. He walked the stairs slowly. Bitter she'd left the dining room, but when Jamie entered their bedroom he heard laughter coming from the bathroom. Also, he heard the running water from where Summer was preparing to take a tub bath. He lay across the foot of the bed hoping the bath would calm her. He had learned from his mother that some days women's emotions just flared up like fireworks, and since he did not recall doing anything to her, he hoped that this was just one of those days. He could hear Summer still on the phone while she soaked in the tub. After a while all of the fun and laughter that did not include him became too much for him, so he flipped on the television and was able to catch half a movie before she came out of the bathroom. She had a towel wrapped around her body and one wrapped around her long hair as she walked with one hand clenching the towel and the other holding ever more tightly to her cell phone. "So, you're off the phone," he said in a calm voice while looking away from her. "You and Suzi must have plenty to talk about tonight." Summer responded with a simple "Yep" and walked away to her mirror. "Well, tell me about it," he said while flipping the television off with the remote and sitting up aiming all of his attention to her. In response Summer removed her towel from her head, allowing her long, wet hair to drop as she hooked up her hair dryer and turned it on. The sound of the blow-dryer was drawing out any conversation they could have had, but still Jamie didn't give up. He spoke out louder, saying, "Well, HOW WAS IT!?!" She stood with her back to him flipping her hair side to side.

"HUH!!" she yelled out.

"HOW WAS IT!?!" he got louder.

"HOW WAS WHAT?!?" she yelled.

"YOUR DAY!?!"

"OH, MY DAY?!?"

"YES!! YOUR DAY!!"

"IT WAS NO BIGGIE!!"

"WELL, TELL ME ABOUT IT!!"

"WORK, WORK, AND MORE WORK!!" she yelled, and then she switched the dryer to the highest heat, which also happened to be the loudest level. Jamie sighed to himself. That was going to be his last gesture for the night. He walked to the bathroom, where he proceeded to prepare for a well-needed shower. He let the hot water pour down over his head in an attempt to wash away his stress for the day. By the time he was done, he came out to find his wife lying in bed with her eyes closed. Asleep she appeared, but asleep she was not. Either way, Jamie was done trying to communicate for the night. He grabbed his silk black pajamas and made his way to the living room downstairs, where he watched television until he fell asleep. When morning came, Summer reached over to his side of the bed and had only the plush comforter to comfort her. She popped out of bed, immediately realizing she had not set the alarm clock. It was an hour past her usual wake-up time. If she hurried, she could still make it to work on time, but she was really hoping for an extra hour for grooming. The whole morning while she prepared for her day, she did not see or hear Jamie. After being fully dressed, she placed the final touches on her hair and headed for the door with no breakfast, and she never even called out once for Jamie. She just assumed he went in to work early. When the door closed shut, Jamie appeared in the dining-room doorway. Standing there, his face showed no emotion. His eyes, though, did flicker in thought. He never heard her call his name; she never entered the dining room to see if he was there. How strange, he thought. They both worked that Tuesday. It was just a different type of day for both of them. Jamie entered his office and was greeted immediately as always by Layla with a fresh cup of coffee with one pack of sugar and four creamers, just the way he liked it. It never mattered what time Jamie came in; even if he were late for work or early, Layla would have his coffee ready and fresh. At first, Jamie found it to be strange, but over time he began to accept it with a smile and a thank you. On this Tuesday morning when Layla came with the hot coffee with one pack of sugar and four creamers, Jamie did not accept it. He placed one hand up towards the cup in a stopping gesture while shaking his head no and dropping his chin towards the floor. He made a quick step to the right, where he proceeded to dodge by Layla and head for his office. "Hmmm," Layla slurred as a sneaky grin approached her face quickly. Her smug look remained as she lingered in that one spot gripping the handle of the coffee mug. Finally, she sipped from Jamie's coffee mug and walked away slowly in thought. As the day went on, Jamie continued to mope. Layla, on the other hand, began to plot. When she brought paperwork in to Jamie's office to be signed, she asked him how Summer has been doing this week. Jamie reopened with a "just fine," but Layla was digging for more. Later she rang his phone line with the work purpose to tell him that his appointment for the day called and rescheduled. Layla took the opportunity to snoop further in Jamie and Summer's life. "So what did you and the missus do on your day off yesterday?" Layla threw in before Jamie could hang up the phone. "Summer had to work all day, but I got a chance to get some well-needed housework done." On the other end of the phone, Layla's smile lit up like a cheerfully colored Christmas tree. Ding! Ding! really went through her head. She felt as though the words she was saying were like a shower of gold falling down to the end of her rainbow. Barely containing her emotions, she slightly giggled before saying, "Well if MY husband was off on a Monday, I would have took that day off too so we could spend time together. Well, of course I don't have a husband; just a single woman waiting for that number one man in my life. And when I do snag him, well I mean FIND him, he would never have to do housework on his day off. That would always be taken care of but that's just me," Layla said as her final words before hanging up the phone, leaving Jamie at the other end with the phone still to his ear. He was already in a slumpy mood, so he decided not to respond to any of Layla's thrashing remarks—although Layla took his silence to mean he was starting to see the light and he would soon be hers. In another town, at Slick Ladies Silk, the day was rather quiet for the store business—so quiet in fact that Summer decided to send one of her employees home early. Her pick was Joanne. She told Joanne to enjoy the rest of her day and that she and Jason could handle the store just fine today. The minute Joanne left, Jason approached Summer.

"I really enjoyed talking to you on the phone last night. I am so glad you finally gave me your number. Talking to you on the telephone really brings back memories. I think I like talking to you better on the phone than even in person."

"Now why would that be?"

"Well, you're so light-spirited and open over the phone."

She smiled without showing her teeth while flouncing around the store counter walking past him in her flirty summer dress with red flowers printed all about the white cloth texture. Red was Jason's favorite color, and Summer had remembered. His eyes followed her as she twisted from side to side walking from different areas straightening up the silk items the customers had left astray.

"Yeah, calmer you are. More laughter and straight talk."

"Uh huh," Summer let out as she stroked her hand down a long silk scarf ever so gently and slow.

"I heard splashing water last night repeatedly."

"Yeah, so!"

"Yeah, so what were you doing?"

"A girl has got to get clean, you know."

"Yes, they do. Maybe you can call me tonight while you're splashing around. You would really be doing me a favor because lately I've been having trouble sleeping, and the doctor said I should get a tape of running water or kinda like the ocean splashing on rocks. Yeah, he said it would really relax me. And I know after I got off the phone with you last night, I slept like a baby."

"Is that right?" Summer said as she stopped in the middle of the floor and gazed at him in his eyes from across the room. During lunchtime, Jason decided that it would be a good idea for him to go grab some take-out Chinese food and bring it back to the store, and he and Summer could lock themselves inside and eat together. Summer originally opposed the idea, but Jason quickly convinced her to just leave a sign up on the door saying "out to lunch, will return shortly." When Jason returned with the food, he pulled a table to the front and slid it to the side of the front door, so they would be out of view of customers walking up. Summer went to the restroom to wash her hands for lunch. When she returned to the front, she was very much surprised to find that Jason had prepared the table with one of their finest silk cloths and three little dogwood flowers, which he had picked up outside, in a small cup decorating the center of the table. When he saw her eyes pop open wide and her mouth drop, he began to buff up his chest as if he was extremely proud of what he had done. All was well until she yelled out, "HAVE YOU LOST YOUR MIND?! Boy, get that

$200 silk cloth off that raggedy, dusty-looking table." Jason was just about to put the food on the table when Summer quickly walked up, removed the flowers, and snatched the cloth off while all along mumbling, "Well if you're not going to take it off, I certainly will."

"Summerset, you're ruining the ambiance," Jason said while leaning over and placing the flowers back on the table, while he concentrated on ways to redecorate the table. Summer examined the silk cloth well. "Thank goodness there are no snags from that raggedy table," she told Jason with her forehead knotted up in anger. He took the opportunity to comfort her. He walked up to her, placing his right hand on the small of her back and with his left hand took hers, and he led her body gently to the chair that he had pulled out for her. Her body relaxed, and the wrinkle of anger was swiftly deleted from her forehead. No longer caring about the silk cloth, she allowed Jason to put it away, placing it gently on the showcase nearby. The moment now calm, they both sat and ate. They indulged in conversations from the past. Remembering the times when they were a happy couple and were wondering what would today be like for them if Jason's dad had never moved him out of town. Halfway through their lunch, there was a tug at the door by a customer. Summer inched her body towards opening the door. Jason put one finger to his mouth to shush her while placing his other hand on top of the hand Summer had lying still on the table. Summer did stop moving and sat straight in her seat again. Fighting all of her instincts to try to be a manager and take all the money she could get for one day, she just sat there. The customer walked away after a couple of tugs. They figured she must have stopped and read the sign saying "out to lunch." Summer sat quietly in shame until she heard the car speed away. Then she busted out with laughter and her body was filled with a high rush of relief, like a criminal who got away with a crime. She was filled with excitement as if she had done something naughty. Her body was nervous, excited, and her heart was beating rapidly, all causing her to lose herself for just one moment. In the midst of her excited laughter, Jason went to her. Standing directly in front of her with a solid face and stern jawbone, he called her to him. She was very much intrigued, so she did stand and step forward. He placed his hand behind her neck. She could feel the tiny hairs rise as she began to breathe deeper. Her eyes were his focal point as they faced one another. Preparing herself for what was about to happen, she parted her lips slightly and slowly while all along allowing her eyes to follow Jason's tongue as he licked his top lip, only using the very tip of his tongue. She closed her eyes and let go of all of her inhibitions and she allowed Jason to kiss her on the lips. Slowly and steadily they kissed as their bodies became even more relaxed. He continued to hold his hand on the back of her neck; he also added his other hand to her back, using it to press her body even closer to him. During this time, another person pulled on the store door. Jason heard it, but didn't care, so he continued on. Summer was too deeply involved in the kiss that she did not notice the first tug on the door at all. Jason pushed her up against the wall with his body while he continued his kiss, so they wouldn't be seen. More tugging persisted and Summer noticed this time. She turned her head away, breaking the lock of the kiss, now scared and ashamed. Jason whispered to her, "No worries, they will go away. They can't see a thing. We are in a corner backed against the wall. Only the nosiest of persons could see us." The minute he said that, the tugging at the door became more intense and the voice of a woman was yelling out, "HEY, LET ME IN!! I came a long way just to pick up something from THIS store! YOOHOO!!" The lady continued on while peeping deeply from the side of the door through a little square glass. "I see you back there, you know! Come on and open up! Is this a place of business or what?!" Summer slid herself on the floor and crawled away from Jason a bit before she stood to open the door, so it wouldn't seem as if they were too close to one another. When Summer did open the door and saw who stood on the other side, she wished she had never unlocked it. Her body physically and visually trembled from fear. She had imagined a hole appearing beneath her feet and swallowing her whole and she falling out of sight. "Out to lunch, huh," the woman spoke out to Summer as she glanced at the table in the corner with the plates, flowers, and half-eaten food. "Don't seem like you're out to lunch to me." Summer, with watery eyes and trembling voice, spoke, "Layla?! What brings you all the way to Saratoga?" A snappy-toned Layla responded with, "The question is, why is there an 'out to lunch' sign on the door when lunch is clearly in?" She said this with an attitude while looking directly at Jason, who was still standing against the wall near the table. Jason spoke to Layla, "How do you do, ma'am, how can we help you?" "WE," Layla projected, "so when did you two become a 'we'?" Summer, feeling panicky and sick to her stomach, stood still, not knowing what to say or what Layla would say to Jamie. Jason stepped out of the corner and explained to Layla that he worked there and if she needed something from the store, he would be more than happy to help her find it. "If you really want to help me, you can explain to me why when I peeped through this window," she said as she pointed at the glass behind her, "why did it look like you two were standing in this corner together. What could you have possibly been doing standing that close?" Jason was now starting to get very irritated. His patience for the noisy customer had ended. His voice rose as he pointed back at her, saying, "What we were doing is none of your business, lady!" He was prepared to say more, but Summer quickly snapped out of her fearful haze and jumped in between them before Jason, who had no idea who Layla was, said something that might cause all of them pain later.

"Layla, I'm sorry for the new employee's attitude. He is working on customer service." She turned to Jason and called him by his last name, asking him if he could go count the inventory in the back room. He did walk away, but not without him and Layla staring each other down until he was completely out of sight. "Layla," Summer called out to direct her attention away from Jason, "I'm sorry you had to see this setup in the corner, before we were finished working on it. I'm trying to design a little showcase area. I wanted to put a couple of mannequins in the chairs having lunch with silk scarves around their necks." Summer turned and grabbed the silk cloth Jason originally had on the table. "Yeah, I'm even thinking of laying this nice cloth over the table. What do you think?" Summer said as she stretched the cloth out in front of Layla, praying in her own head that it would distract Layla's mind.

"You want to know what I think?" Layla asked.

"Yeah, sure," Summer said with a fake smile while still

looking at the silk cloth. Layla in turn smiled and she said, "I think this has been the best extended lunchtime I have ever taken." She looked in Summer's eyes and Summer looked back. Layla detected fear and she loved it. She began to laugh for no known reason towards Summer. She shook her head and walked out of the store still laughing. When the door closed shut, Summer grumbled. She had slowed the expensive silk to hit the ground. Jason entered back to the front at that moment because he heard the door close. He rushed up to pick the silk off the floor. He walked to the showcase and laid it there. He noticed Summer still standing in one spot. He walked up and put his hand on her shoulder. "What's wrong?" he was saying. Summer immediately jerked her shoulder and snatched away from him. She sped past him with anger, never saying a word. She reached her office and Jason heard the door slam. "Well I guess I can take a hint. I'm not wanted right now," Jason said while walking to take the "out to lunch" sign off the door. He resumed store business and Summer stayed in her office for the rest of the day dealing with her own thoughts and holding her cell phone closely in case Jamie called. Jamie was all she thought about for the rest of the day. Questions trampled through her mind. What was Layla really thinking, although she pretty much made her thoughts obvious? What would she tell Jamie? Would she tell him anything at all? Thoughts like this carried her head until closing time. She stayed in her office all day. When it was time to leave, Jason came to her door and tried to get her to come out so he could see her safely to her car. She yelled back at him, "No, I'm much too busy in here with paperwork. I have been neglecting my paperwork all week, I have tons of it. Please leave without me." Jason tried turning the doorknob to the office, but he found it to be locked. He stopped twisting the knob and pleaded with her one more time to come out. Again she said no, so Jason walked away mumbling, "I know when I'm not wanted," and he left the building. Summer waited a few minutes in her office to make sure Jason was good and gone. She came out of the office and went around tidying up the store. She went to the little table where they had lunch and cleared it. She placed the silk cloth back on it. Summer went to the back and even managed to find two workable mannequins for the display she was designing since she had told Layla about it; she wanted it done in case she mentioned it to Jamie. Summer worked on the display until it was almost perfect. One little thing is missing, she thought, a couple of nice wigs for the mannequins. Summer looked at her watch and it was an hour past the time she usually left. She grabbed her keys and rushed to the door. She still had almost an hour drive home ahead of her and she still was not on her way. Jamie was always home before her even though they got off work at the same time because he did not have as far to travel. Summer stopped a moment when she got to the door. She turned and looked in the corner where she had the new display. Summer was shaking her head and clenching her keys tightly as she remembered what had happened in the corner. Opening the door and easing out of the store, she glanced up and saw the two bald mannequins and shame rushed over her once again. Her eyes dropped to the ground as she closed the door completely and began her journey home. The whole ride home she thought about Jamie. Her biggest concern was what would Jamie think about her getting home an hour late if Layla had mentioned anything to him about her and Jason being alone at the store today with the building locked up? There would be no excuse for that, she thought. "Jamie knows how I feel about closing the store even for lunch breaks," Summer said as she began to talk aloud to herself in the car. "Even when I am the only one working in the store, I always call in an order so I can keep the doors open and I have told Jamie this. He has even seen for himself when he wanted to take me to lunch and I waited for Joanne to get off of her lunch break before we left, so the store would be covered. I told him that day, 'you can't make a dollar with your doors closed.'" She took a deep breath and sighed hard before saying her next sentence. She yelled out into the car where she sat alone. "Now how in the world do I explain two employees in the store with an 'out to lunch' sign!! UUGGHHH!!!!" she yelled out with extremely high anxiety. Halfway home, Summer's phone rang. It was Jamie. She saw the Caller ID and heard the special ring tone that she had set just for him. She panicked. She didn't know why he was calling and she didn't know what he might have heard, if he had heard anything. On top of that, she didn't know what to say to him. She did not answer. A minute later her voicemail alarmed. Long message, she thought. "I wonder what he said." No matter how much she wondered, she still did not check her voicemail. She was too scared it was a bad message. Jamie had never left her any bad voicemails. Only sweet, humorous ones, so she was not yet prepared to handle a change. Fifteen minutes later, the phone rang again. Again it was Jamie, and again Summer refused to answer it. Another voicemail was left, which seemed even longer than before. Summer decided not to listen to either message. She would soon be home and she would face whatever she was about to face. She thought if she did not answer the phone, her relationship would be safe and intact. She and Jamie would stay a happy couple as long as they never spoke of this day. When Summer pulled into the yard at home, she saw Jamie open the door quickly. He was coming towards her with a look of devastation on his face. She soon formed a face of fear—her anxiety was heightening as she watched him running for the car. She swallowed hard and closed her eyes tightly just before Jamie jerked her car door open, calling her name. He was grabbing her by the arm and pulling her out of the car. She didn't know what to expect next. When she was finally on her feet, he grabbed her quickly and held her tightly, almost sobbing when he called her name once more.

"Summer, you're okay. I was so worried," Jamie said in the most intense voice.

"Yeah, I'm fine, no worries. I'm only an hour behind schedule."

"I couldn't reach you on the phone and I got this anonymous call saying there had been this terrible accident along the same path you drive, and that some woman that fit your exact description may be dead."

"Seriously! The street was the clearest I've seen it in months. I was hoping to pass a couple more cars, so I could know I was still awake."

"Well whatever the situation, I'm glad you're safe." He loosened his grip he had on her and stepped back, giving her room to breathe. "Let's go in the house, you can tell me all about your day," he said with a smile while taking her by the hand. Summer, now aiming for the house door, had her eyes open wide and half of her lip underneath her teeth with as tight of a grip as she could bear. When they got in the house, Jamie led Summer to the living room. They sat together without even flipping the television on. They sat together on the couch. Summer kept quiet at first and leaned towards the coffee table, where her fingertips almost reached the remote before Jamie snatched it up and tossed it to the loveseat. He smiled hard at her after doing so and said, "All we need is you and me." Just as Summer feared, the next question out of his mouth was one of his usual ones. "So, tell me about your day." She wanted to roll her eyes in the back of her head, but didn't in fear that she would really tip him off to the problem. Instead of rolling them, she batted her eyes and put on the biggest baby doll smile and leaned in towards him, placing her hands on top of his. She whispered with powder soft lips that were covered with her favorite cherry ChapStick as they were inches away from his own lips. "My day was fine," she said softly, "but do you really wanna talk right now?" She said this with the biggest attempt at distracting his mind. It was working well. He did lean in with no more intent to talk. His lips had just graced hers when just that second a double beep cracked the silence. They both paused with lips still attached. It was Summer's phone. It was not a ring, but it was a text message signal. Summer feared to look so she ignored it and pressed her lips more to Jamie's. BLEEP, BLEEP! The double beep had alarmed again. Jamie pulled away, unlocking from the kiss. "Uhm, I think that's your phone." Even more afraid that if she looked, he would look; what if it is him? she thought. Jamie would see, and what did he say that would be seen by Jamie? More nervous now that her phone alarmed for a third time, she lounged herself on top of Jamie as he fell backwards and his head hit the arm of the couch. "Ouch!" he cried out. Still she continued pressing up on him and trying to kiss. This force of attention from his sweet, laid back Summer alarmed him. He turned his head away so she could not plant her kiss. He slid his body away and up. Now standing, he noticed her phone alarming for a fourth time. "Hand it here, I will check it for you if you'd like." Hearing those words made Summer's heart bounce so hard she did a double-take, looking down to her chest to make sure it did not pop through her shirt. She didn't move or speak, but words did go through her head at one hundred miles per hour trying to process what her next move should be. If she snatched it and ran, that would be no good, she thought. Before Summer was forced to act, she was saved by the ringing of Jamie's phone…or so she thought. Closing her eyes with relief, she held her phone with both hands tightly toward her heart. She took a deep breath of relief and was calming down when Jamie answered his phone and turned his back to her. All was perfect for a split-second as she peeped at her phone and was just about to delete the messages even before she read them, but that split-second only caused a double drought in Summer's world when she saw Jason's number attached to the text messages, and then heard Jamie say aloud, "Layla, what's up?" Jamie began taking steps away as he spoke with Layla. Summer went blank with her phone in her hand. Thoughts from Summer: *Now!?! Not now. Please, Layla, not now.* Jamie talked aloud to Layla on the phone while Summer listened. "…never hear from you this late. What's new? No way!! Can't be! What makes you think that?" Jamie asked while walking further away from Summer. Summer could barely contain her emotions. Real tears were falling down her cheek while she listened to Jamie's conversation and saw him moving further away from her. Jamie entered the dining room, and Summer could no longer hear the conversation which was devastating her to the core. A moment had passed, and Summer saw Jamie walking back into the living room with an aggravated look on his face. As he approached her closer, her mind snapped and focused. She made a quick glance at her phone and swiftly she deleted the text messages without even a chance to read them. *Oh no!* she thought, *here comes disaster on the way. How do I explain my way out of this one?* Now standing directly in front of her with a heavy face, she felt as though her heart had fallen clean to the soles of her feet. When she heard her name called aloud by Jamie, fear filled her up. She wanted to cry or even faint, but she didn't. "I can't believe this. How could this have happened?" Jamie said with a tone of anger that Summer had never heard him use. He twirled around away from Summer, placing himself close to a small table in a corner where he slammed his hand down hard just before saying, "I don't know what I did to deserve this." *Here it is*, she thought. She opened her mouth and began to say "It really wasn't…" Before she finished the sentence, Jamie turned to her and softened his demeanor.

"Baby," he said, leaving a look of confusion on Summer's face.

"Yeah," Summer reluctantly said.

"This is so crazy, but tomorrow morning I gotta be on a plane to San Francisco."

"What? Wow! Really? Why?" she asked, while not really caring why he was ACTUALLY leaving. Really she was just relieved the attention had not turned to her.

"My oldest and best client has decided he wants to drop our agency and go fresh. He thinks a new agency will put a different spin to his products. I can't believe this. I'm beating my head against the wall trying to figure out what I might have done wrong on his last project for him to want to leave me. My marketing agency can't afford this drop, it would be major. I'm going to have to go to San Fran to do my best to woo him back before he goes with the new guys. I hear the new deal goes down in two weeks. It gives me very little time, but at least I have some time left. I'm glad Layla called to give me a heads up on this thing. I'm not real sure how she heard about it this time of evening, but I never second-guess Layla's connections. She's great sometimes. It was her idea for me to get on the first flight to Cali and try my best to make this all better." Summer lingered for a moment before asking, "So that's all Layla called for?" "Yep I guess, so what else would she be calling for?" "I don't know. Calling this late, I just figured…," a babbling Summer said as she just let the last word die out slowly. She dropped her eyes to the floor and started nibbling on the inside of her jaw quietly. He looked at her. "I know what's wrong with you." She immediately popped her eyes up towards him and awaited his response. "You're worried because this will be our first time apart. I'm so sorry about this but I will try and call you as much as I can." "Don't worry about me. Just handle your business. This is very important so take care of things and don't worry a bit about me. I have plenty of work to keep me busy at the shop." "Thanks, baby, for understanding; you're great. I gotta go pack; Layla has already booked me a flight and set me up with a hotel for me. Can you believe it?" he asked while walking up the stairs. Now at the very top he yelled down in laughter, "Sometimes it's great having a secretary!" Summer twisted her lips and responded with a low-toned "umm humm, yeah they're just great."

The very next morning, Jamie was ready by 6 a.m. and on his way to catch a seven o'clock flight to California. When Summer arrived in the parking lot at Slick Ladies Silk, she had her mind made up to tell Jason that she was completely done and yesterday was a big mistake. While Summer was in her parking lot space, she observed Joanne and Jason's cars side by side. She sat in the car an extra few minutes gathering words for when she got the chance to talk to Jason alone, and also gathering her face and words for when Joanne would see her. Summer didn't want Joanne to detect any funny business. "Okay, Summer," she said, talking to herself out loud as she got out of her car. Walking to the door, she took the deepest breath she could before walking into the store. When she entered the first person she saw was Joanne. Summer put a big fake smile on her face just before saying good morning. "Morning," Joanne said with a groggy voice just before taking a sip of her coffee. Summer quickly picked up that Joanne wasn't in a talkative mood this morning, but it was perfect timing for Summer because she wasn't in a talking mood either. Summer walked past Joanne and headed for her office. She felt she was almost home free, but then she saw Jason walking out of the storage room. Summer said hello. "You are in a little late this morning." Summer wanted to just keep walking without saying a word. She did not want Joanne to notice and start asking questions so she did respond. "Yeah my husband had a business trip. He left this morning," she said while dropping her head to the ground. She kept walking past. Summer never even looked up at Jason. She made it all the way to her office and closed the door. She did not wait to hear a response from him. Summer later felt herself to be lucky when the workday went on to be extremely busy, leaving no time for talking between any of the store employees. Come lunchtime things did calm down, but Summer felt that was okay because she still needed the time to talk to Jason alone. She wanted to make things clear to Jason, so today she asked him out to lunch. He accepted with a grin on his face. Summer told Joanne that she and Jason would be taking first lunch. She did tell Jason they would be driving separate cars. "What about car pooling?" he asked. "Car pooling is out today. I have plenty of gas," Summer responded while she grabbed for her own keys. At lunch, Summer did not order much like she usually did. She only had a salad, which she did not even put any dressing on, and a water without her usual lemon. Really she had no appetite and did not plan to eat, but she did not want to look silly with an empty place set. As soon as they ordered and the waitress walked away, Summer proceeded to give Jason her speech which included how happily married she was and that she could no longer play teenage games with him. She ended her speech by saying they were just friends and he would have to accept that. Jason listened to everything she had to say and at the end of her speech he said, "I accept your terms and will be a lucky man to have a friend like you." Summer felt so relieved hearing him say that. Then she exhaled, smiled, and relaxed. Also, she waved the waitress back to the table and told her to add a baked potato and a steak well done to her order, and also a few lemons in a cup on the side. They both found the rest of their lunch to be very pleasant. Jason watched Summer enjoy her last bite of steak, looking pleasantly satisfied. "You really seem to enjoy a good meal," Jason said. "While I was in New York I went to a culinary arts school for a couple of months. I really learned how to cook some fine cuisine. I would love to cook for you one day this week. Didn't you say your husband was out of town? No buts," Jason replied. "I just want to treat you for all you have done for me. You know, giving me a great job and all when I needed it. Friday night: great dinner, great company, and I promise to be good." Summer's mind was saying "bad idea," but her mouth said, "Okay, but as long as you remember what I said here today. I guess it couldn't hurt anything," Summer said. Their lunch ended and they headed back to the store. On the drive back to the store Jason's cell phone rang and it was Summer. She told him to just let this dinner thing be between the two of them and he agreed.

The next day, Summer went to lunch alone. She spent her time shopping for an outfit to wear Friday. She figured if she was having fine cuisine, she should look fine right along with. She tried on three different outfits and none of them were perfect enough for the occasion. She left the store empty-handed and went back to work. Halfway there she remembered a dress Jamie had brought her from Paris. It was long, silky, and red. Red is Jason's favorite color, she thought. She'd never even worn this one yet because it was so beautiful; she wanted to wait for the perfect situation, time, and place. This was it, she assumed, so she made plans to try the dress on again as soon as she got home. Work seemed to have gone by slowly for Summer; she figured it was because she had plans for when she got home. The workday did come to an end, and she found herself at home rambling for that perfect dress of hers. She found it, disrobed from her work attire, and placed the dress on her body. The dress comforted her every curve as it held to her skin. She smiled and nodded to herself as she eyed her own body in her full-length mirror. "Purr-fect."

Summer spent the rest of her night in a teenage-like trance. She was lying in bed when she got a text. It was an address. Jason had just given her his address to prepare herself tomorrow night. Another text message came in reminding her not to expect him at work in the morning because he took the whole day off to prepare his fine cuisine. Summer melted more in her teenage trance as she read the text messages over again and admired the smiley faces. Her phone rang and the trance was broken when her husband Jamie's name appeared across the screen. She answered and they held a great conversation, but not once did Summer mention to Jamie any of her plans for the next day. When that next day did arrive, she did wonder early that morning whether she should have mentioned the planned dinner to Jamie since after all it was harmless. They were absolutely and totally just friends now. She quickly let all thoughts of Jamie out of her head as she prepared a bag for the night. This bag held her dress, makeup, supplies, extra deodorant, and even an extra-clean pair of red underwear. Summer went to work dressed in blue jeans and a t-shirt with her hair wrapped in a ponytail. She hadn't dressed so plain for work in quite a while. She didn't mind dressing homely for the day for she knew by evening she would be dressed like a princess. At work Joanne questioned Summer about why Jason was allowed to take a Friday off of work. After all,

Friday was one of their busiest days. Summer jumped to Jason's defense as she told Joanne about all the days he had been at work without any absence, and he had come to work early and stayed late days. Joanne had no real entrance in Summer's response. She walked away, waiting until she was behind Summer and completely out of sight before rolling her eyes in circles. "Whatever" also crossed her mind.

An hour before closing time Summer sent Joanne home early. After she had driven away, Summer placed a closed sign on the store door. She skipped to her car and grabbed the book bag that carried her supplies for the evening. She went to her office and laid all the supplies on her desk. She went to the bathroom, which was connected to her office, and freshened her entire body with wet naps, which she kept in her drawer. After her cleansing, she rubbed her body down with baby oil. She went back to her office desk and placed her clothing on her body. She went in her desk drawer, where she peeled out a beautiful antique-looking hairbrush with a silver handle. The brushing end was wide and strong—perfect for Summer's long, thick hair. She stroked her hair with the brush for a while before reaching back into the desk drawer to retire a back at her hairpins. She pinned her long hair and left only a side piece hanging from the right. After applying her makeup she headed out; her next stop would be Jason's house.

Standing outside of Jason's home door dressed to her finest, Summer contemplated turning around. *No,* she thought, *maybe I shouldn't do this.* Her thoughts continued for a moment. *Even though it's just dinner, maybe I should have talked to Jamie.* She pinched the sides of her dress, raising it up a bit from the ground and revealing her newly worn high heels so that she might walk with ease down his steps. She began walking down with a shake to her head as she heard many words pass through it. Summer had come to the conclusion that this was something she should not do, so she turned to leave without even knocking. Before her heel could click on that last step, she heard another type of click; it was the front doorknob turning. Jason was pulling the door open. "You came…," Jason said with a cheerful voice. Summer smoothly twisted her body towards his direction. She raised her head up and parted her lips to say, "Yes of course, that WAS the plan……right?" She clicked her heels right back up the steps as though it had been her first tour up. This time she made it all the way in his house. He stood back three big steps before closing the door or asking her to have a seat. He glared at her with a grin and nodded approval as the sun from the open door caught that red dress on fire. He glared as the rays from the sun seemed to have pointed out vivacious curves, taking his mind to places that he had only traveled in his dreams. Standing in silence a bit too long, Summer became uncomfortable, so she spoke to break it. "Should I have a seat or do I have to stand during dinner?" Jason said, "No, please, do sit. Dinner is almost done. I just want to put some final touches on it before you see the dining room. Sit and relax, I'll be right back." Summer glanced around the house as she sat there amazed that the place was so upscale. The living room had a fireplace and a chandelier. Jason had told her that funds were so low that he had to move to lower-grade housing. If this was lower grade, she wondered about where he had moved from. Jason entered the room, interrupting her thought with a rose in his hand. She stood to her feet and looked at the rose. "No thanks, you keep that. No roses needed for a friendly dinner," she smugly said as she walked past him peeping around for the dining area. Jason stood as she walked past him and admired her arrogance among other things. He thought, *fiery red dress with a fiery red attitude; only lights my fire.* Jason tossed the rose on top of the fireplace and headed behind her. Summer admired the dining room. The first thing that caught her eye was a chandelier over the table.

"Another chandelier? Is there a chandelier in every room in this house?"

"Just a few, it used to be ceiling fans, but I had them all replaced. What can I say, I love the glamour of a chandelier."

Summer thought it to be strange that he could afford to do all of that when he was in such a financial strain when moving in, but she kept that thought to herself. She saw such a delicious-looking dinner on the table, she didn't want to ruin the evening with complicated chatter. Jason went to the end of the table and pulled out a chair for her; she walked over and took her place. Jason walked to the other end and sat in front of his plate. Jason had his fork halfway to his mouth when his bite was interrupted by Summer tapping her fork on her water glass. With his mouth open wide and a fork of prime steak only one inch away from his mouth, he looked up at her and froze. "We should do grace over our food," Summer said with a questionable look on her face as she wondered in her own mind why he never thought of that. Jason put his fork down and told Summer she could have the honor. She blessed the table and was left feeling empty. Jason never noticed that she was disturbed. He was busy shoveling the food down his throat. Summer ate slowly while she tried to decipher the emptiness after the prayer. Before Summer took her last bite of food, it came to her. The emptiness for her was caused when she said a prayer over a dinner that was not only without her husband, but in another house with a man who fantasized about her. *Who am I kidding?* she thought. She also liked him a little as well. Her stomach began to twist from nerves. She figured the guilt was chewing on her insides. She pushed her chair back and rose from her seat. "How was it?" Jason squeezed out with a stuffed mouth. "It was just great. Truly fine cuisine, just like you said." Summer said this with a low tone and a straight face. She began walking out of the dining room while saying, "I better be getting home now." The words alarmed Jason. He started strangling the water he was sipping. He put the cup down hard, splattering drops of water. He scraped his chair backwards quickly and propelled his body out of his seat. He stood and said, "Don't rush. I rented a movie. It's one of your old favorites. I know your husband is not home, must be lonely." She paused and considered what he was saying. "Well it does get a little lonely 'cause I stay up pretty late. I will watch the movie and then I'm going straight home," Summer said as she took a seat near the television. "That's fine by me. Whatever you want; let me pop this movie in." The movie was starting and Jason took his place on the couch right beside Summer. This made Summer very ill at ease. Jason sensed this and played it to his advantage as he reached his hand up on her shoulder. He gripped it firmly but gently while telling her how tense she seemed. Normally, Summer would have pushed him away with no hesitation, but the repeated gripping was relaxing. So she just sat and said nothing. Jason appreciated the silence. He took this as a signal to slide closer and add his other hand to her other shoulder. "Yes, very tense," he said. "A nice massage is sure to relax you. Just watch your movie and relax." Summer told herself if she just sat quietly, she wasn't doing anything wrong. She never said go ahead with the massage, and she never said stop either. Her silence was sweet melodies to Jason. In his mind, he was given a pass to freedom. "You have such beautiful hair," Jason said as he eased his hand to the top of her head and removed one hairpin. He stopped for a moment and waited to see: would the feisty Summer that he knew snap him up for his attempts. Still she sat watching the movie as though nothing was happening and she was completely alone. Jason tossed the hairpin on the table and continued pulling the rest of the pins out. Soon he had a bundle of hair flowing between his fingers. Strong and thick, it empowered him. He gripped it tightly and he felt her body tremble. Even more empowered now, he held the grip and pushed her head directly to his head. His lips touched her lips and they did explore one another. Feelings of fresh excitement were all over Summer's body. Soon her mind snapped her back to her reality. She pulled away, unlocking the kiss. "I'm married," she said loudly, as if she was trying to convince herself more so than Jason. Jason backed his hands completely off of her. He leaned in towards her ear and softly told her that it was okay because no one would ever have to know. "NO! I must go," she said while jumping up from her seat, but never taking a step towards the door. Her heart said "go," but her body said, "please stay." Her mind said, "I only need a little more convincing." Jason stood in front of her and became very serious when he put her hands into his hands and looked into her eyes. "Stay with me just this one time and I promise you no one will ever have to know. I will never tell, and I know you won't. We dated for years in high school and you never gave me this chance. I feel like since we were together so long, we deserve a memory like this." He noticed the silence take over Summer again and he was pleased. He persuaded her to come and see his room upstairs. "No home tour is complete until you see the bedroom," he said. When she entered the room, it was no surprise to her when she saw a chandelier over the bed. *Isn't that a bit dangerous*, she thought, *a chandelier hanging right over you at night, but who am I to say anything*, she thought, because the whole game she was playing tonight was dangerous. When Jason entered his bedroom, his aggression went up tenfold. Before Summer knew it, her pretty red dress was lying at the foot of the bed. For a split-second she thought about stopping him and asking if he had any protection, but she decided she did not want to interrupt the moment. If she was going to be bad, she would go all the way. Besides, she said to herself, he's right…no one will ever have to know. So she lay back and let the moment of the night wash over her.

Five o'clock in the morning, Summer's eyes popped open wide and flashes from the night took over her. At the time it was all wonderful, but now that a new day came, she felt sick. She ran to the bathroom and vomited. Tears were coming from her eyes and she felt as though her heart was crashing. Jason heard the noise and entered the bathroom to see if she was okay. Ashamed, she snatched a towel and covered herself. Running past him, she yelled out, "I can't believe I did this to Jamie!" She twisted the towel tight around her and snatched her keys off the nightstand and stumbled to her knees, grabbing her dress. She ran down the stairs as Jason called out to her. She never turned back; she slammed the house door behind her and vowed to never return and to never betray Jamie again.

When Summer returned home, she showered until the hot water ran cold. She hoped that the water would wash away her sins and shame. She left the shower drenching wet. She entered her bedroom without even toweling off. The water from her hair fell to the ground fast as did her tears. She lay on her bed in the silent house and she wept. She hoped that the silence would not last forever, but her husband's voice would fill the void soon. She knew that if her husband ever heard of this past night, the silence would continue forever and so would the weeping. Her weeping continued through the early morning until she fell asleep across her bed from exhaustion. About one o'clock that afternoon, her house phone rang and woke her. When she answered it, it was Jamie panicking from the other end. Her heart raced when she heard the tone of his voice. She feared he knew already, but she relaxed for a moment when she found out he was only concerned because he could not reach her on the phone all night. The relaxed moment did not last long for Summer. She was quiet on the phone trying to figure out how she would explain missing all of his calls. Summer told him she was sorry, but she left her cell phone in the car all night, which was a true statement. Jamie then asked how she missed the ringing of the house phone. That one puzzled her for a second, but she knew she could not linger with an answer because he would think she was lying. "Well, I went to bed early last night. I was soooo tired from work, I'm not sure if there was something wrong with the phone line and it just didn't ring or was I just too exhausted to wake up. As a matter of fact, I do think I heard the phone ring, but I just thought it was a part of my dream. You know how I sleep, just get so dazed out sometimes. I'm so sorry, but anyway how are you and how are things going with the business deal?" Summer said to divert Jamie's mind far away from her. Jamie calmed down and told her he had been struggling, but he thought he had almost convinced the company to stay with his marketing agency. He told her he would be home Monday. After the phone conversation was over, Summer felt bad about lying to Jamie, but she did not know what else to do. Summer was glad it was the weekend. She had no work and Jamie would not return home until Monday. Summer felt that she needed this time to herself to straighten out her mind and to figure out what she needed to do to make it all better. Summer stayed at home all day Saturday. She tried to keep busy by organizing everything she could think of. She cleaned all of the closets in the house and even washed clothes that were already clean. Her plan was to keep busy and she would not have time to think, so she thought. Halfway during the day as she leaned on her knees in a closet, her cell phone rang; it was Jason. She did not answer. She told herself she was completely done with him. She knew now that they could not even be friends. She picked up one of her favorite shoes and threw it to the back of the closet. She was angry at Jason for calling her. She was angry at herself because she did not answer. She was angry that all the work she was doing was not keeping her mind off of this disastrous situation she had caused in her own world. She got up off her knees and went to the kitchen for a snack. Her day had been long and her stomach was empty.

She fixed herself a bowl of alphabet soup, one of Jamie's favorite things to eat with crackers. She sat at the table with her soup, waiting for it to cool. She looked over at Jamie's empty chair and could not stop the tear that fell from her eye. She began stirring her soup to cool it off, but she found herself playing in the soup, searching for all the letters that would spell out "JAMIE." She figured it was a good thing that all she had on her mind now was her husband. She did take small comfort in that. She had almost calmed herself enough to take a bite when she felt her phone vibrating on her hip. She removed it from the clip and became angry all over again when she saw Jason's number appear. *He has to stop this*, she thought; *what if Jamie was here?* Summer let the phone ring and again did not answer. Jason never left a voicemail. Summer sat at the table now, unable to eat her soup. She came to the conclusion that she would have to talk to Jason one more time. She would have to tell him it was over. She sat holding the phone in her hand, hesitating to call Jason's number. She took a deep breath and hit the button. Now her phone was calling the last number that called her, which was Jason's. Summer's breathing went to a fast pace and her posture was stiff and stern at the table. She heard his voice say "hello," but no words came out of her mouth even though it was open. "Hello…Summer?" She heard the voice again. Taking a deep breath and letting it out over the phone, Summer decided to speak.

"Please don't talk, just listen. Last night was a big mistake and can never happen again. I DO love my husband." When she heard the words come out of her mouth, she stopped to receive them. *Yes it was true*, she thought, *I really DO love my husband*. Again she said aloud, "This was a mistake."

Jason spoke up and told her he understood how she felt but he still wanted them to be friends. "If you want to be just friends, I can accept that; but please don't shut me completely out."

"I am sorry, but I can't accept that. From now on, our relationship will be strictly professional. Nothing more," she said before hitting the end call button on her phone. Feeling slightly satisfied with herself after the conversation, she sighed from relief and began eating her now cold soup. She did not get up to warm it. She figured there was no point because today she would remain cold on the inside and nothing would warm her.

Saturday floated away slowly for Summer, but soon she woke with the rise of the Sunday morning sun. Summer was still wrestling with her conscience. She felt she needed someone to talk with. She feared talking to anyone for several reasons. She didn't want them to tell Jamie and also she did not want them judging her. Her heart still weighed so heavy. She needed to talk to somebody for fear that she would explode. She gathered her things and headed to the church that she was married in. Bishop Carlton was old, wise, and would never tell someone's conversation. She went to the church, but did not go in for the service. She waited outside until service was over and she saw people clearing out of the parking lot. She had heard that Bishop Carlton always stayed after church and sat in his office to meditate. She waited to get out of her car until she saw all but one car leave. Bishop Carlton was still in there. She walked into the church and went straight for his office. She raised her hand to knock, but she suddenly hesitated. The door pulled open and there was no more need for knocking. Bishop Carlton stood at the door in his robes with his Bible in hand like he was heading out. It was much to his surprise to see Summer standing on the other side of the door.

"If it isn't Mrs. Summer Garnett. Well I don't think I have seen you since your wedding."

"Well life has had me a little busy, Bishop," Summer said while bowing her head in shame.

"Not meaning to lecture you, my dear, but God has blessed you with health to be busy; don't wait before he slows you down to make time for him," Bishop Carlton said in his elderly and wise voice.

"I might have made a mistake coming, Bishop. I think I should be going," Summer said as she turned from the door.

"Please wait, come in my office. Sit, and let me explain myself." Summer entered the office and sat in front of the bishop's desk. "Well let me start over. I am so excited to see you again. I have heard stories from others that have had the opportunity to spend time with you, members of the church. They felt so encouraged just by your presence. I just wish we had that encouragement around here more often." Summer was delighted in hearing that she had touched the lives of others even though she was still unsure how. "When we fellowship together, we encourage one another. So I hope to be seeing you here a little more," Bishop said with a chuckle. "I'm sorry, I have just been talking your ear off. I know you must have come here for another reason." Bishop Carlton got quiet and leaned back in his chair, crossing his fingers over his belly. He took a deep breath and told Summer he was listening.

"Well Bishop, I really need to talk to someone and you came to my mind. What I have to say is serious and hurtful. I need your word that you will never speak of this conversation to another soul. And…if you can, please don't judge me."

"You have my word. I'm not here to judge you. We all need to work on getting our lives together before God judges us, and if talking to me in confidence is one of the things you need to start ordering your steps in the right direction then I am more than willing to oblige." His kind words comforted and encouraged her to speak. "Okay…I have betrayed my husband in one of the worst ways. The way of adultery. Now I have been through some trials in my life but I don't know what to do now. This time is different. This one has been the hardest for me." She paused for a moment before continuing and looked up at the bishop to see if he had a face of disgust. He didn't. He only had a face of concern, so she continued her story. "It's so devastating what I have done. I caused this drama," she said as many teardrops fell from her face. She held her hands down under her chin, cuffed them together as she caught the tears in the palms of her hand. "I caused this rain on my own life." She balled up her fist as the tears melted away. Bishop Carlton walked beside her and put his hand on her shoulder. He stood there allowing her to shed her tears. He did not try to speak with her but only to be there and to comfort her. Summer appreciated it. She felt it was just what she needed at that moment. He prayed over her and welcomed her back at any time. He gave her his home phone number. Summer left the church feeling better. She called Joanne and told her to run the store Monday. She was going to stay home and await Jamie's arrival. Summer went home. She cleaned a little more, ate a little dinner, and went to bed early.

Jamie's Return

5:35 a.m., Summer woke to the sound of her front door opening and items being tossed around. Startled and frightened, she grabbed the phone. Her fingers fumbled over the wrong numbers, as they were shaking from fear. All she got was a dial tone. She heard running up the stairs and suddenly her bedroom door opened. She grabbed her pillow, hugging it tightly while screaming. Her eyes wired shut. She was too afraid to open them to see who or what was standing at her door. On top of her screaming, she heard yelling. "It's me! Surprise, I caught an early flight home." It was Jamie talking; she stopped screaming and opened her eyes slowly. She opened them one at a time with only a little peep to be sure the voice she heard was Jamie's. When she was sure it was him, she loosened the grip she had on the pillow and slung it across the room, hitting Jamie in the head; she cried and yelled in hysterics, "Never scare me like that again!" He only stood there and laughed. "Man, I missed that," he said while smiling and shaking his head, and she calmed down. "You missed what?" she asked. "You, and everything about you," he replied. (Summer and Jamie had a great Monday together. Jamie had kept his client and Summer was enjoying having her husband at home. Summer felt as though everything was perfectly normal. She enjoyed herself as if nothing had ever happened. Denial was just what she needed to feel better about her life, so she thought.)

Tuesday morning Summer arrived at work early. She wanted to get there before everyone else so that she could arm herself mentally before Jason got there. It was much to her surprise when Joanne came to work and walked directly to her, reaching out a letter. "What's this?" Summer asked.

"You won't believe it! Go on, open it," Joanne said with a frustrated face. She stood there allowing Summer to read the letter. When she was sure she was done, she spoke up and asked, "Can you believe this? Now we are right back to being shorthanded around here again." The letter that was given to Summer was Jason's letter of resignation. Summer was shocked to see it, yet pleased. "So, he just left this yesterday?" Summer asked Joanne.

"Yep, and strange thing is he worked all day and never mentioned it. Thirty minutes before closing time he gave me the letter and said to give it to you with his apologies, but he's gonna be moving back to New York next week. He got a new job already and all! Strange, very strange. I think that man has more money than he lets on," Joanne said to Summer.

"Yeah, that is strange," Summer said as her mind traveled back to the chandeliers. She soon let the thought go and walked away smiling. She felt good. She thought in her head, *This is perfect, he moved all the way to New York, now no one ever has to know and I don't have to see his face every day and be reminded of the whole mess.*

Joanne was irritated because now she thought it would be harder for her to take days off work now that they were back to two employees.

Three weeks had passed since Jason left and Jamie returned. Summer was very attentive—as good as when they were first dating. On the weekends Summer made Jamie's breakfast and dinner, which was a switch from their usual routine. Jamie was loving it. He was not sure what really changed Summer's attitude back to the way he liked it, but he had an idea. He thought it had something to do with him going out of town. He remembered the old saying, "Absence makes the heart grow fonder."

One day Summer was on her lunch break at a little café sitting at a corner table alone, enjoying a burger while reading her favorite book. All was calm until she peeped up from her book and saw a lady standing in front of her. Summer thought it was her waitress, but to her surprise it was Layla. Summer placed the book over her face in hopes that Layla would go away. When she heard the chair across from her slide out and Layla sat down without an invite, Summer knew what she had hoped for was only wishful thinking. Summer lowered her book and laid it on the table. She looked up at Layla and said, "Oh, Layla, it's you, won't you join me for lunch?" "No time to be coy," Layla said. "I'm here strictly on business." Layla was not one for beating around the bush. "What, Layla?" Summer asked.

"You cheated on Jamie, and I'm going to expose you. That's all I really came to say," Layla explained and then busted out in a psychotic-like laughter. Summer's face tensed, but she stayed calm. She thought to herself, *Layla only saw us having lunch or maybe standing a little close, but I can explain that with my display.* After Summer had convinced herself, she spoke up and told Layla she did not know what she was talking about. "Oh you don't?" Layla asked while placing her big black purse on the table. She reached inside and pulled out an envelope. Summer just watched in silence. Layla pulled out a picture. She turned it towards Summer and it was a picture of the outside of the diner where she and Jason usually ate their lunch. Noticing that neither she nor Jason was in the picture, she got bold enough to say, "So you have a picture of a diner, so what?" Summer replied with an attitude. Layla had a smug look as she placed that picture back in the envelope and pulled out another. This time Summer's heart began to beat a little faster. When Layla turned the picture around for Summer to see, Summer noticed again that neither her nor Jason was in the picture, but she still became afraid. This picture was one of Jason's front door, and she could recognize her own car in his driveway. Now Summer was not so bold to speak. Layla smiled at her silence and placed that picture back into the envelope as well. She spoke and said to Summer, "Now I only have one more picture left, but don't worry: the last is never least. You're going to love this picture just as good as you did the others." Layla smiled and laughed a little more as she reached for her last picture. Layla stood from her chair and held the picture tightly. She lowered the picture just enough for Summer to see it. Summer saw and then put both hands over her mouth and her eyes got watery. The picture was clearly one of her in front of Jason's house leaving out wrapped in a towel with the red dress Jamie gave her in her hand. Layla responded to Jamie's watery eyes by saying, "You see, I told you you'd love it." She quickly put the picture away and turned to leave the café. Summer spoke out to her. "Please don't do this! It was a mistake. It's over now and it will never happen again." Layla turned and looked at her with a puzzled face. "Yes," Layla replied, "it is definitely over," and then she left the building. Summer was left inside and she felt like it was her prison. She could have left at any time, but she felt like a convict who had been incarcerated too long and was now afraid of what life would be like in the outside world. She stayed there longer than she should have. It was way past her lunchtime. She stayed and tried to think of a solution. There was none that she could come up with because Layla held all the cards. She was in charge of what would happen next. Summer did wonder why Layla waited three weeks before she approached her with this. She thought, why now when things at home are going better than ever?

Summer felt it was time to call in reinforcements. In light of the new situation, she felt that she was going to have to involve her best friend Suzi. Only she and Bishop Carlton would know about the adultery. Summer felt that she could trust the two of them to keep her secret in a nonjudgmental way. Summer got on the phone and called Suzi to come and meet her at the café. She told her to hurry, that it was an emergency. She said she would tell her everything when she arrived. Summer's next call was to Joanne. She told her she would have to run the store alone for the rest of the day. She told Joanne something had just hit her hard and her stomach was doing flips, which was no lie at all. Joanne agreed to cover for her, and she wished her well soon.

When Suzi got to the café, she rushed in wearing blue jean shorts and a tank top, and she had her hair pulled back in a ponytail. She glanced about frantically looking for Summer. Summer raised a hand so that she could be seen. Suzi darted over to her and demanded to know what was going on and was she all right. Summer assured Suzi that she was all right physically, but needed her to calm herself and prepare for a serious mental issue that was at hand. "I rushed right over just like you said I should. I thought I was gonna have to help you fight or something. I got my hair all pulled back and my sneakers on," Suzi said in a joking way as she placed herself in the seat in front of Summer. Little did she know that joke was almost a reality. Summer quickly told Suzi about everything that had happened, even down to Layla's threats. Then Summer was quiet and waited to hear Suzi's response. "Well where is this girl? We need to find her and have a little chat." Summer was relieved to hear Suzi respond in her usual fiery way; this meant to her that Suzi didn't think any less of her. "No, it would only make things worse," Summer responded to Suzi's statement.

"Then why did you call me all the way down here then? We could have had this conversation over the phone. I can't believe we are just gonna let some psycho chick spy on you, for who knows how long, and threaten you, without even having one pleasant conversation with her," Suzi said just before beginning to leave the café. Summer spoke out as she saw her friend leaving. "Don't tell anyone!" Suzi replied back with a smart "yeah yeah" as she threw her hand in the air and exited the café. Summer did not feel any better after telling her friend; in fact she felt worse. She dragged herself out of the café (which she somewhat feared leaving); she started her journey home and hoped that none of the juice from the café had spilled out to Jamie.

Summer made it home before Jamie for once, due to leaving work early. She fixed him some alphabet soup and some crackers and had it hot when he walked in the house. He entered the house and bubbles of anxiety reached her chest. Jamie walked directly to her before speaking. While standing face-to-face she was unsure of the look he was betraying. She was sure of one thing: it was not his happy face. "You won't believe what happened today. I really don't even know how to tell you this." Jamie began mangling his words, for he was uncomfortable about what he had to say. He turned and started walking from side to side, no longer able to look in her face. Turning his eyes away from Summer caused her chest to be filled with even more anxiety. Her whole body was begging to anticipate upon the words that would soon spill from Jamie's mouth. She felt paralyzed with fear. The air in her lungs felt less and less. She couldn't concentrate to stand still and be calm. Her mind bounced from thought to thought, also causing her heart to bounce harder as well. The vibrations from her nervous body began to scare her. She just knew if he did not say what he had to say soon, she would have a heart attack. Jamie continued to walk and dawdle without words; Summer finally called her body at attention and told herself to calm down. *This was no heart attack*, she said to her dancing insides. *Only a small panic attack. Whatever Jamie saw will not kill me. I must stay calm and in control.* She took a deep breath and let it go slowly. Her pulsating body began to calm. She was able to speak. "You need to just get it out and tell me what's going on," Summer said with a bolder attitude. "Okay, but sit down 'cause this is going to knock you off your feet," he told her.

"No, I won't sit, whatever it is I will take best standing." That's what Summer said out loud, but she was really thinking she had better stay on her feet in case she had to run.

"Okay, well, I'm just going to say it, Suzi came to my office today." When Summer heard that news, she really could not imagine what would come next. "Suzi? In your office?"

"Yes, and she said some mind-blowing stuff." Summer stayed silent, wondering did Suzi, could Suzi really have outed her secret and told Jamie everything? Suzi was never the predictable type so Summer remained calm to hear from Jamie what Suzi really said. "Okay, I'm just going to say it. I know I said it before, but this time…okay…" Jamie stood completely and looked her in her eyes. "Suzi tried to get me to sleep with her." Summer thought back on when Jamie told her to sit down. Now that option was looking necessary. "You know I think you were right, I should sit down." So Summer did sit, but she was flabbergasted. Not knowing what to say or what to think, her face had this look as if she had bitten something sour. "You don't need to worry, I told Suzi I would never cheat on my wife. I also told her that she should be ashamed of herself. She is supposed to be your best friend. I wouldn't let her get another word in before I threw her out of my office. I'm sorry," Jamie announced as he laid his hand on her slumped over shoulder. Eventually Summer emerged from her mind-blowing state and she and Jamie had a few fake laughs over the situation. On the inside, Summer was like a ticking time bomb. She was sure that when she had the opportunity to get to Suzi, she would explode. Meanwhile, Summer thought, Jamie was in a pretty good mood considering the situation; this meant neither Suzi nor Layla had mentioned the affair to him. Later that night she heard Jamie say that Layla was on vacation for the next two weeks. He also said she was already out of town. Summer knew for sure Suzi was not out of town earlier today. She wondered did she really have plans out of town, or did her plans consist of lurking around and spying on her more? Summer couldn't understand what Layla was up to. Layla had information for Jamie, but she had not told him a thing apparently. Was she really planning on exposing her, or did she only want to hold something over her head. Another thought popped into Summer's head, but this one she said aloud: "Maybe she just looked at her shaking her head. Yeah, I don't know what's up with Suzi." Her mind flickered for her outburst. Suzi? Her mind flickered for a split-second, Oh yeah, Suzi, she thought. I don't know where her mind is.

Summer told Jamie that she needed to go out for a while. She said she would stop at a store and get them some snacks. What she didn't tell him was that she was also going to make a pit stop to Suzi's house as usual like all was well. Summer did walk on the inside but would not sit. She was hoping Suzi would just tell her everything without her ever having to say a word. It did not happen. Suzi offered Summer a drink and even wanted her to stay and watch a movie. Summer stood at Suzi's door mesmerized by Suzi's sudden memory loss. After being silent for a while, Summer figured enough was enough. "No, this is not a social call. I'm going to need to know right now why you, my best friend, tried to sleep with my husband," Summer blurted out. Suzi calmly, boldly, and seriously responded, "Well, you just told me you didn't love him anymore, and I always did think he was cute; so after all you said, I figured you wouldn't mind."

"WHAT!" Summer yelled out in rage. "I never told you I didn't love my husband."

"All that stuff you told me earlier clearly stated that you didn't love him anymore. I have been knowing you for years and you would never cheat on someone you loved. I am your best friend! If I knew you loved him, I would have never done that," Suzi said with all sincerity.

Summer stood in astonishment. "Are you for real?" Summer asked Suzi.

"I never told your secret" was Suzi's response.

"I can't deal with this, stay away from my husband, stay away from me." Those were Summer's final words before slamming the door behind her.

About two weeks later on a Monday morning, Summer was lying in her bed. Suddenly her eyes popped open wide. The first thought in her head upon waking was the name Layla. She leapt from her bed, and her body knelt over as she grasped both arms around her stomach. Summer was literally sickened by the thought of Layla returning back to work. She jetted to the bathroom. On her knees she gagged with the thought of Layla. Jamie heard the noise and he rushed from the bed and was promptly to her side to console her. He instructed her to take deep breaths, seeing how she was only gagging and nothing was coming out. She soon calmed herself for Jamie's sake. She did not want to worry him. When they left the bathroom, they sat side by side quietly. Jamie rubbed her back to comfort her. She noticed that he started smiling rather boldly and brightly. This puzzled her. A smile in the midst of her sickness was not like him. She turned to him and just gave him a look that asked him why without sounding a word, why? He laughed out loud before responding to the look. "Nauseated, mood swings, I think I finally figured out what's going on. You must be pregnant!" Jamie shouted. As soon as the words hit the air and floated to her ears, Summer began gagging again. She hopped off the bed and ran for the bathroom, this time slamming the door behind her. Screaming commenced in her head. She screamed to herself, *Pregnant! He thinks I'm pregnant; he is happy thinking about a future with me and as soon as he gets to work, there is a woman waiting to crush and burn our relationship. Uggggghhhh!* she screamed out in her mind while gagging continued out loud. Jamie convinced Summer to stay home from work so she could rest and feel better. She tried convincing him to stay with her. He told her he had a big business week to prepare for, and he really needed to be at work, and so he went to work.

The first person he saw when he got there was Layla of course, approaching him with his hot coffee. "How was your vacation, Layla?" Jamie asked. "It was great, I visited family and friends that I haven't seen in years, but most of the time while I was gone, I thought about you. We really need to talk," Jamie heard and figured she was up to her old tricks of trying to land him for a date. He walked away from her, telling her he had to prepare for a big meeting that he would be having next week. He said he did not have time to talk as he kept walking past her. He sighed as he closed his office door, saying quietly to himself, "I thought she had all of this silliness behind her since I've been married."

Layla sat at her desk feeling more impatient than ever; she had waited to tell Jamie anything in hopes that Summer's own insecurities and fears would worsen her own marriage before she told. Plus, the whole situation gave her a sense of power and control, which she hadn't had in her life in years. She did love it, but now she felt she had waited long enough. She must let Jamie know so he would leave Summer, and then Jamie would soon be hers forever. Layla couldn't concentrate on work. She twiddled her fingers for a while and prepared her speech in her mind, which she knew he would not believe her if she told him with no proof. The pictures of the restaurant, Jason's house door with Summer's car near the house, and Layla's personal favorite, Summer wrapped in a towel holding her dress—they were all safely sealed in a white envelope. Still Layla stayed seated, imagining her chance to talk to Jamie. She played with the sealed envelope, sliding it through her fingers from one hand to another. Deviously she sat grinning and thinking. She heard an office door open, and she quickly hid the envelope in between the other mail that was all waiting on her desk in need of sorting. Work that had been left on her desk while she was away. Jamie came up to her and asked her to pull a file for him on a Mr. Davis. "Yes, sir, I will get that for you right away," she said before leaping out of her seat in a nervous manner. She brought him the file quickly. He took it, but he also reached down and picked up the stack of mail on her desk.

"Oh, sir, that's just the mail. I can sort that for you."

"Yeah I know, I'm sorry, I actually left this mail on your desk. I meant to take these off your desk before you got here," Jamie said as he walked away, leaving behind a very dismayed Layla. She stood in place wondering what she should do, or even if she should do anything. No, she thought. This was perfect. He would open all the mail to sort them and when he opened that one, he would fall apart and run straight to her arms so that she could pick up the pieces. The smuggest look she'd ever presented fell upon her face. She stood nodding her head in acceptance of the idea of Jamie finding the deception himself. She waited an hour later and she heard nothing. She decided to have patience, so she continued to wait. Soon it was lunchtime and still nothing. Jamie came by her to leave for lunch and he didn't mention anything. She was left confused. While Jamie was out, she peeped in his office. Looking on his desk, she couldn't see the mail. Now even more confused, she walked back to her desk and she waited for Jamie to return. When he walked in, she immediately asked him had he finished sorting the mail? He told her he'd reviewed the names on the letters days ago and decided they were not worth opening. "I just dropped them all in the shredder without another look," Jamie said with ease as he walked back to his office. When she heard Jamie's office door click closed, Layla reached both hands up to her head, grasping a handful of hair on each side. Her mouth opened wide as she silently screamed with no one else in sight. After a while, she calmed down only slightly and decided that though her evidence was gone, she would still have to confront Jamie and tell everything she knew. *All is not lost*, she thought. "Maybe he can still be mine," she said aloud with a smile.

After much contemplating at her desk by the end of the day, Layla had planned what she would say to Jamie word for word. Jamie came out of his office all prepared to go home. He was stopped by Layla. She told him his wife was having an affair. Jamie quickly became angry, his nose flaring and his teeth grinding together. He could tolerate many things, but he refused to let anyone slander his wife's name. He told her in the strongest tone he had ever used with her, "NO, IT'S NOT TRUE!!"

"I got proof," Layla said.

Jamie stopped for a moment and his eyes widened. "What proof could you possibly have?" he requested.

"Well, I HAD proof," she said in a low tone with her head dropping as she felt she was losing her power. Jamie, now even more enraged from Layla's lies, turned to leave.

"WAIT!" Layla cried out in one last attempt. She ran to his office, ripping his shredder out of its socket. She dragged the shredder to the front and poured it all on the floor. Frantically, she searched while Jamie watched and assumed she was crazy. "It's here!" she cried while trying to gather all the fine pieces of paper together to recreate her evidence, but it wasn't working. It was too destroyed. Jamie began to walk away again.

"Wait!!" Layla yelled out once more. "I followed her for weeks. I saw the restaurant where they ate together."

"Men and women eat, Layla. She has a male employee!" Jamie yelled.

Frantically Layla yelled back as Jamie's foot was almost out the door, "I saw her coming out of his house in nothing but a towel." Jamie stopped. Layla could not see his face, only his back. She took a relaxing breath. *Good, he stopped. Now he sees that Summer is bad for him and he will turn and cry in my arms. Once he finds comfort in my arms, he will never leave*, Layla thought. Jamie did not turn around, though. Also, he did not yell. He was now completely calm. His voice lowered when he told Layla that they could no longer work together. He told her she should clear out all of her belongings immediately. He explained that her attitude at work was not professional or acceptable and her last check would be mailed to her. When Jamie finished talking, he put his paused step in motion and left the building, never looking back at Layla. Layla, still on the floor covered in shredder paper, cried while feeling like her insides had also been destroyed by the shredder. Gathering her things was hard for her, but she did. The pain of losing Jamie forever weighed hard on her heart. Layla packed and left town that night. No one in the town ever knew what happened to her and no one ever saw her again. Layla left town because she knew if she ever saw Jamie again, no matter where, she would fall to his feet crying and begging for him to be with her; but she knew that this time while she was down there, he might kick her. Her heart could no longer bear the pain. She knew she had to find a way to move on. Also, she knew if she ever saw Summer again, no matter where, there was no telling what she might do.

At the Garnett home, Summer was worried sick because Jamie was late getting home and he had not called. She feared Layla had spilled the beans.

The ride home for Jamie was a bitter one. He thought many things, such as: Why Layla'd had to take her obsession for him so far as to lie on Summer? He had decided that he would never tell Summer about Layla's lies. He trusted his wife, and even bringing the conversation up would sound accusing. Jamie entered the house and Summer was waiting for him on the couch. She didn't speak when he came to her. She waited to see what he might have to say to her, may it be good or bad. She noticed some kind of look on his face that was not his usual, but she could not pinpoint its emotion. He wasn't saying anything either so she figured she would speak.

"You're home late," she said.

"Yeah, I got held up by Layla," he told her. She stood from her seat, very afraid. Jamie followed by telling her that he had to fire her. Summer reluctantly asked him why. He sighed and told her that it had been a long time coming and he thought the stress of working for him had finally gotten to her. He walked away from Summer and went upstairs to his room, thinking what he'd just told Summer was the truth and hoping that she did not ask for more details. Little did he know, he didn't have anything to worry about. Summer was too afraid to ask more, even though in her heart she felt that Layla had told him everything.

Eight months had passed since deception and unfaithfulness had reared their ugly heads in the Garnett's home. Jamie was still in disbelief about the truth, and Summer was unclear on why Jamie never approached her, but they lived the eight months together. They appeared to be somewhat happy again. When things felt too peaceful or happy, Summer would get a little sad because she would remember the secret she held from Jamie. Summer was still glad that she had made it. All seemed calm in her relationship. Jason was gone. There was no more cheating. Suzi never told Jamie anything about the affair, and if Layla did tell, then Jamie either didn't believe or refused to acknowledge it. Either way, her marriage was still going and she was happy.

Back at work, Summer's boss had returned from her trip. Summer was no longer manager, but she didn't care. Things were much more peaceful this way. One workday, Summer returned from her lunch break and was approached by Joanne.

"You had a call while you were out."

"Who was it?"

"It was Jason."

"Jason who…?" Summer asked just before she felt like her heart had dropped down to her feet.

"You know, our old employee, Jason. He left this number for you to call him back," Joanne said while reaching Summer a torn white paper with his number. Summer hesitated to take it. Joanne told her it was okay, and that he probably just still thought she was the manager. Maybe he even wanted his job back. Summer took the paper, saying, "Yeah, maybe," and she walked away. She walked to a trash can and tossed the number inside. Her workday was ruined. She continually thought about Jason. She did not know why he was calling but she assumed he wanted her. Things with Jamie were going well, and Summer would not break her vows again. Where was he? she wondered. Hopefully still in New York. She didn't need him popping up in their lives again. She swore to herself that she would not return his call. The next day he called again, but this time she was the one who answered.

"Slick Ladies Silk, where our silk is the finest, how may I help you?"

"Summer, this is Jason. I'm in town and was wondering if we could meet for lunch."

Caught off guard, Summer responded rudely. "No, never, and don't contact me again." Then she slammed the phone down.

The next day, she was at the store alone while her boss and Joanne took their lunches. To her surprise, Jason entered the front door. She became angry. She did not greet him with a hello, but only with a hateful "What are you doing here?"

"I'm sorry. I need to talk to you and you hung up on me."

"Well, maybe you don't understand the meaning of a dial tone, so let me explain. When made on purpose, it usually and most likely almost always means that the person on the other end does not want to talk to you. Therefore, showing up to talk to them in person is a moot point," Summer explained to him with all the feistiness she could muster up.

"Look, I need to speak with you about something very important. Please come to lunch with me."

Summer was sticking to her "no" this time. No one would ever make her break her vows to Jamie again. "No lunch, no conversation…now get out!" she told him.

Jason himself became angry this time. "I was trying to be nice and understanding about this whole thing, but I have had enough. Where do you get off with this holier than thou attitude, because if I'm not mistaken, when I woke up, you were lying in MY bed! I was not there alone," Jason announced to her.

Now infuriated, she yelled out into the empty store, "GET OUT OF MY LIFE!!" And so he did leave and he never returned. A month later, Summer received a letter from him in the mail that was sent to the store. She was so glad she had never given him her home address. As she held the letter in her hand, she was very tempted to toss it in the first trash can she saw without reading it; but she didn't. Instead, she put the letter in her purse and saved it until her lunch break. She went to the park and she sat on a bench that had a perfect view of the apple tree in front of her. She gazed upon the dormant apple tree and its hard dry winter stems. Summer thought about how the change of a season affects all things. The same apple tree she admired in the summertime for its beauty and fresh produce, now, in the wintertime, drew up and shivered with the cold. Her thoughts distracted her mind as she delayed on opening the letter. She figured there was no real need for dawdling, so she focused and opened the letter. She read:

Dear Summer,

Wow, this is crazy. I don't even know your new last name. Anyway, I made a strong effort to tell you this in person. You asked me never to contact you again and I almost honored your wishes, but I had to honor the times we were close friends. It was long ago, but I hope some day in your heart, you can remember me fondly. Although after I tell you why I am writing you, I am sure any fond memories of me will soon be forgotten. I ask you in advance to please forgive me. I'm taking this time to acknowledge my sins and ask all that I have wronged to forgive me. There are some things you don't know about. First, I never lost my house in New York; and I never lost my job. I own my own business in New York, and I have other people running it for me. I basically pop in and out as I please, so I had plenty of time to venture to other cities. When I first went to Slick Ladies Silk, I only wanted a job so I could hit on women. I didn't know you worked there until I saw you. When I did see you, old feelings came back and I knew I had to have you. So I begged you for a job and I lied to you about my poverty. Again, forgive me. I wish this was the close to my letter, but I do have one more thing to say. I don't have any easy way to say it. I'm just going to write it bluntly. I went to my doctor because I had what I thought was just a cold that would never go away. She ran some random tests that meant nothing to me at the time…until I was called back to her office and was told one of the tests came back positive. There is no graceful way to put it…I have HIV. Things have turned for the worse for me. In my adult life, I have been bouncing from one woman to the next. I do not even know who I got it from. Like me, they probably don't even know they have it. I never had an HIV test. I never thought it could happen to me. I waited too long to find out. My immune system is extremely low. I didn't know I had a problem, so I have not been taking my medicine. I just found out my HIV has advanced to full blown AIDS. (*The tears began streaming down Summer's face as she read the harsh word "AIDS." She tried to continue reading but the words were blurry as her tears blinded her. She wiped the tears and read on.*) My doctor told me I had to contact all the women I had ever been with. They all needed to be tested themselves. The list is long, and at this moment, it saddens even me. I'm sorry you're on my list… (*The letter ends!*)

Summer stayed seated on the cold bench; her hands gripped the letter that was now covered with her tears. Her eyes were directed back to one word that could destroy her life forever…AIDS. She stared at it, written in all caps, allowing it to stand out over everything else. She looked at the word until she could no longer see through her tears. With a grip upon it tighter than before and wet from so many tears, the letter lost its strength and began to tear as did Summer's heart. Summer's tears, mixed with the bitter cold breeze, numbed her face, while she stayed seated on the bench. She thought the cold must have also numbed her legs as she felt paralyzed to move them. The temperature outside became colder. A harsh gust of wind rushed her face, taking her breath away. It was just what she needed at the time to snap her out of devastation. She stood from the bench, drying her tears and encouraging herself to move to her car. She made it to her car and started her engine, but she couldn't bring herself to put it in motion. Next, the shock of the news hit her and she screamed at the top of her lungs inside the car, body twitching as she grasped the idea that she might this death sentence. Finally, she told herself that just because he had HIV did not mean she had it. After what seemed like an eternity, she got on the phone and made an appointment to see her doctor in the morning. The gesture caused her to calm her mind. She went back to work to keep busy. She told herself she wouldn't worry until she got actual news to be worried about. Summer worked hard that evening. She stepped up fast any time she heard the store door open, so that she could be the one to help. Even when there were no customers, she stayed busy with cleaning, stocking, and other things. The time came for her to go home and she found herself staying busy at home too. She also had an added chore at home that included avoiding Jamie, which worked out well seeing how Jamie was also busy. He had brought home some paperwork that needed his attention. Nighttime came and they were both exhausted. They soon fell asleep. Morning couldn't have come soon enough for Summer. She had taken the whole day off for this doctor's appointment. She arrived an hour early. It did not get her seen any quicker, but her mind could not focus on being anywhere else. She was delighted as well as fearful when she heard the nurse call her name to go to the back. She felt she had waited long enough. She needed answers. Summer felt she went from one waiting room to another. Even though she was now in the examining room, she continued to wait. After twenty-two minutes, Summer was relieved to hear a tap on the door. It was the doctor finally. Summer explained to the doctor that she only wanted some routine tests done, which included all the sexually transmitted diseases. The doctor sent a nurse in who asked all the usual questions about Summer's sexual background. Then she got a sample of Summer's DNA and left the room. Summer waited a little more, then the doctor came back to the room and told Summer it would take three days for the test results on the HIV to come back because the doctor office had to send it away. Summer was upset. She did not want to wait any longer, but she had no choice. She left the doctor's office in a slump. She was glad she'd taken the whole day off. She went home and slept all day. Jamie was at work thinking his wife had only gone to the doctor for a routine physical. He was completely oblivious to the fact that his wife had an underlying purpose for her visit.

The three days was miserable for Summer. She stayed so busy that when the day came for her to receive her results, she was physically drained. On this day, the doctor was the one to call her to the back. The doctor took Summer to her office to give the results—she said so she wouldn't hold up any of the exam rooms. She prompted Summer to have a seat and asked her did she bring anyone with her or did she come alone? *Strange question*, Summer thought before telling the doctor that she came by herself. The doctor named Summer's tests one by one and the word "negative" followed behind them until she got to the final test. She paused for a moment before she said, "Summer, you tested positive for HIV." Summer placed her feet in the doctor's office chair. She balled up fetal position in the doctor's chair as she heard the news. Her arms draped across her knees. She held them tightly for comfort. She cried helplessly as her mental capacity could not handle the horrible news. The doctor knew that this was not going to be a good time to explain the disease to her and her options from here. She wanted to speak with her when she could better understand and interpret the situation. The doctor stood from her desk and walked to Summer. She placed her hand on her back and told her she was sorry. The doctor walked out of the room and sent a nurse in to comfort Summer and to tell her that the doctor needed to see her back again tomorrow. The nurse called a cab that sent Summer home. Summer lay in her bed. She cried all morning and cried all evening. By the time Jamie got home, her tears had subsided, leaving her eyes red and puffy. Jamie asked about it and she told him she was having a bad allergy attack and it was nothing for him to worry about. He didn't believe her story, but he was not going to pressure her. He only went to her and held her in his arms and whispered softly, "I can feel your pain. If you need to talk, I'm here. If you need a hug, I'm here." Her tears ran again from hearing the sweet words. She wrapped her arms around him and he held her closer. She couldn't stop the water that leaked from her face. Even though he was oblivious to Summer's problem, he continued to support and comfort her.

The next day, Summer called her boss. She told her that she was having a family emergency and needed to take her vacation immediately. Once that was taken care of, Summer found herself brave enough to go back to the doctor. The doctor was glad to see that she had returned. She took Summer back to her office and talked to her. She started off by saying, "With today's new medicines and technology, HIV is no longer an immediate life sentence." The doctor took her time and explained things to Summer. "HIV is a virus that causes Acquired Immune Deficiency Syndrome (AIDS). It lowers your immune system. There is treatment, but no cure." The doctor could see that Summer began losing it again, so she jumped in and told her, "There are general care tips that could cause patients to live years longer." After listing much knowledge to Summer, the doctor told her the most important thing was going to be family and friends. A good support system would help her greatly. Her doctor told her that she would have to contact anyone she had been with physically. Somehow this stunned Summer. She was so far caught up with her own feelings that it never dawned on her that she might have passed it on to Jamie. "I know you're married," the doctor said. "Have you told your husband?" More tears formulated as Summer shook her head "no."

"Well you need to go home and tell him as soon as possible because he needs to get in here to be tested."

With a quivering voice, Summer told her doctor of the affair. "You see, he was never supposed to know," Summer sadly told her doctor.

"Well, I'm sorry, but this is a life or death situation so he has the right to know everything," the doctor told Summer in a hard, judging way. She stood from her desk and walked to the door. Her last words to Summer being, "Summer, he needs to know soon." Then she dashed away from the door, returning to her other patients and leaving Summer alone with her thoughts.

Summer went home. She prepared to tell Jamie everything when he got home. When he walked through the door, she was ready. "Jamie, I have something to tell you," she announced.

"Me first," Jamie said with a popping smile on his face. "Since you started your vacation, so did I. Now we can spend it together!" he excitedly said while holding his arms out to embrace her. Summer told herself this week would not be a good time to tell him. No, she wouldn't give him bad news on his vacation. Soon after the vacation, Summer decided. It was still not a good time to tell him because his birthday was coming up in three weeks.

Summer wanted to do something special for Jamie's birthday, so she started planning a surprise birthday party. She worked hard on planning the party. She focused on perfecting the smallest details. She ordered napkins online that had Jamie's initials on them. Summer concentrated on fixing up a good party. The more she focused on the party, the easier it was to suppress her problems and pretend she had none. Summer was in a state of denial that she took comfort in.

One evening before dinner, while Jamie went to the store for drinks and dessert, Summer sat at home reviewing her list of party preparations. She wanted to call someone to discuss the party with, but this was usually Suzi's department. Summer almost picked up the phone and called her when she sadly remembered they were no longer friends. Summer still picked up the phone. She decided to call Joanne instead. Joanne was surprised to hear from

Summer. It was not often that Summer called her about non-work-related subjects.

"Hi Joanne. I have been planning a surprise birthday party for Jamie. It's been two weeks of hard planning. I think I got every last detail down to perfection, even down to the guest list. I invited all of Jamie's friends and coworkers. I invited his mom, but she won't be able to make it, church convention or something," Summer shared with Joanne.

"Well, sounds good, sounds like you have everything under control," Joanne responded.

"Yep, well one thing though. Mark, one of the guys from Jamie's marketing agency. He got a new girlfriend that he will want to bring along," Summer told her.

"That shouldn't be too bad. I'm sure she will be pleasant," Joanne replied.

"Yeah. Just that she is the only one on my list that I don't know and I want this to be perfect."

Joanne paused for a few seconds, remembering that Summer had not invited her to the party yet. Summer must have picked up on the vibe and she quickly interrupted the silence with an invite to the party.

"Sure, I would love to come," Joanne happily answered.

"Well great! It will be a pleasure having you there. You will be like the only person there that I really know," Summer said with a chuckle. "I gotta go, Jamie just pulled up outside," Summer said while hanging up the phone without a response from Joanne. Summer tucked her list away in her purse and sat on the couch waiting for Jamie to enter. He came in bearing sweets, drinks, and a smile. They enjoyed a great dinner and a nice evening together.

Soon it was birthday time. Summer woke up happy. She

slipped out of bed before Jamie woke up. She prepared him eggs, grits, toast, bacon, and poured him a glass of orange juice. As she placed the food on the table, Jamie appeared in the doorway with a big grin on his face. Summer in turn smiled back at him.

"You're awake?" she stated as she poured his orange juice into his favorite glass.

"Yes, I am, the smell of good cooking and the sweet perfume of a beautiful woman always makes me rise," Jamie stated.

"Sit down and enjoy your breakfast," Summer told him.

"But there is no food here for you," Jamie announced with a questionable look.

"I'm not hungry, and I have a busy day ahead of me. You eat and enjoy. You're the one who has to work today. I'm taking the day off so I can get some areas done around here," Summer said.

"I'm only working half a day today. I know it's my birthday, but I just got a couple of things that need my attention this morning," Jamie said.

"That's fine," Summer told him as she rushed around him cleaning after herself. Jamie ate slowly while watching her darting from one area to another cleaning. It was not her norm and he was getting suspicious, but he sipped his orange juice and kept his mouth shut. After breakfast, Jamie prepared himself for work and headed out the door. This was one time Summer was glad to see him go. She ran out to her car when she was sure Jamie was long gone. She popped the trunk and began carrying party decorations into the house. She worked all morning on decorating and preparing party finger foods. She fixed meatballs and placed them on silver platters for appeal. There were also cheese blocks, cut up ham sandwiches, and chicken wingettes. She had toothpicks in the cheese and meatballs and more toothpicks on the side that could be used for the sandwiches and the chicken. When Summer had the house all set up, she started calling all of the guests to remind them that they needed to be at the house by two o'clock because Jamie would be home about three. She wanted all her guests there and in place to yell surprise.

When the guests started arriving, Summer became anxious. She paced the floor and peeped out of the window every time a new car arrived. She wanted to make sure Jamie did not come home early and ruin the surprise. Summer was looking out of her window when Mark's car pulled up. She was very curious to see what his date looked like. Mark got out of the door for his date. When Summer saw the woman who stepped out of the vehicle, she knew that Jamie would not be the only surprised person at this party. Summer was in shock to see the lady that was walking up to her front steps. The doorbell rang and Summer reluctantly opened the door. "Doctor Jean," Summer spoke out as she stood face-to-face with the gynecologist who'd given her the news about her HIV. "Barbara, please call me Barbara," the doctor told Summer. "Good, you ladies have already met," Mark said as he squeezed past the ladies and entered the party, leaving them standing there alone. Barbara leaned and whispered, "So have you told your husband yet?" Summer could feel the hairs on the back of her neck rise as she slowly answered, "I'm working on it."

Barbara decided to take a seat because she knew Summer was getting tense. Summer left the party room for a while.

Guests were wondering what happened to her. Joanne didn't know what was going on; she was confused. It was almost three o'clock, and Jamie would be home soon. Joanne walked to the stairs, tempted to go and get Summer. Before Joanne could go up the stairs she saw Summer coming down. She noticed Summer was upset and her face was wet from tears. Summer had not yet seen Joanne watching her from the bottom of the stairs. She was startled when Joanne called up to her asking was everything all right. Summer's eyes blared open and focused on Joanne. She jerked her hands up to her face quickly, drying her tears. Summer forced a smile on her face just as she passed Joanne, saying, "Everything is great." She walked to the window right on time. "Jamie is here!" Summer yelled out to everyone. A guest asked her if they should turn out the lights and hide. "No," she told him. "I'm sure he sees all the cars outside." Then the crowd giggled a little, which set a cheerful mood just before Jamie opened the front door. "SURPRISE!" they all yelled.

Jamie's eyes darted around the room at all of the smiling faces that were aimed at him. Jamie's energy was exerting from his body as his smile grew wide and he turned and snatched Summer close to him for a hug. Summer was relieved to see that Jamie appreciated the party. She was not quite sure how he felt about surprises. Jamie pulled away from Summer and started mingling with his guests. Summer went into the kitchen to bring out some hors d'oeuvres. On her way back from the kitchen, she noticed Mark walking up to Jamie holding his new girlfriend by the hand. Summer pushed through the crowd. "Excuse me, Excuse me," Summer said to the many people as she bumped by them dropping little pigs in a blanket along the way. She rushed up in front of Mark and Barbara, cutting their path off from Jamie. "Oh, I'm sorry, were you guys trying to get by that way?" she asked them. "Yeah, I just wanted my man Jamie to meet my new lady, Barbara," Mark told Summer as he tried to walk past her. "Wait! Would you like an hors d'oeuvre?" Summer asked as she practically shoved the tray of pigs in a blanket in Mark's face. Again she had blocked his way. "No thanks," Mark said as he dipped past her, pulling Barbara past as well. Summer and Barbara's eyes met as Barbara was being pulled towards Jamie. Barbara's eyes portrayed a slight smile, for she knew that Summer was blocking the way because she did not want Jamie to meet her. Summer's eyes also portrayed an emotion as she stared into Barbara's eyes: FEAR! Yes, Summer's eyes screamed out fear and her pounding heart was begging Barbara "please don't tell." Summer was hoping Barbara could hear all that her heart and eyes were screaming, but she knew that was a long shot.

Finally, Mark had made it to Jamie. Summer stood back watching with widened eyes like she was looking at a train wreck. Her ears were more focused than ever, and almost like a vampire's, her hearing had heightened. She could hear their conversation across the room. "Jamie! Happy birthday, man!" were Mark's first words to Jamie.

"Thanks, so who do we have here?" Jamie asked as his eyes were averted to Barbara.

From across the room, Summer's body became even more tense than she thought possible as she felt strong pulsations all throughout her being. "This fine lady here is Barbara. My new girlfriend." Barbara laughed. "'Girlfriend' seems like a word for teenagers, we should really come up with a new term for dating people," she said, causing them all to laugh a little. "Well, it is nice to meet you," Jamie said to Barbara. "Yes, it is wonderful meeting you as well."

"Actually, Jamie, you should already know Barbara," Mark said as he cut into the conversation.

"Really? How?" Jamie asked.

"She is the only gynecologist in town! I'm sure she has to be your wife's gynecologist," Mark announced. Summer, who was still listening to the conversation from across the room as people walked by her, grabbed food off the tray she held, as if she were a waitress, heard this and moved up fast. She did a slide step in between Jamie and Barbara, which brought their conversation to a halt. "Pig in a blanket?" she asked with a smile.

"Again, I'm going to have to go with a 'no' on that one. We were just in the middle of trying to find out is Barbara here your gynecologist, you see Barbara can't tell us with the whole confidentiality and all, but I figure she's gotta be since she is the only one in town," Mark said as he filled Summer in on the conversation that he thought she had missed. "Yeah, honey, and the crazy thing is I don't even know your gynecologist's name," Jamie said. Summer did a fake smile and thought carefully. This question was really something she couldn't lie about, she thought, so she told the truth. "Yes, you guys are right of course, because she is the only female doctor in this little town, but back to these pigs in a blanket," Summer said as she shoved the tray up to Mark's face once again. "Why in the world would they call little weenies covered with bread 'pigs'? Don't make me want to eat them," Summer said in the worst attempt to change the subject, but she didn't know what else to say so she figured she would say something silly. It worked too. Jamie smiled, Mark looked at her strangely, and the doctor just shook her head, thinking, *I can't tell her secret even though I want too, I could lose my job, so she should really relax*. After that awkward moment Mark and Barbara walked away and Jamie continued his mingling. The whole party was an awkward, tense situation for Summer, but Jamie and his guests all had a fabulous time together.

The birthday came and went. First Summer did not want to tell Jamie of the HIV because of her shame. Now she was even more afraid of losing everything. Times for her and Jamie had been real good lately, and they both seemed to have been in perfect health even though she was HIV positive. Every couple of weeks Summer had given herself another excuse to why she would wait a little longer to tell Jamie. After four months of keeping her secret, she finally decided tonight would be the night. When he came home she would tell him everything. She was all set this time until Jamie bust through the front door, ran up the stairs, and ordered her to put the warmest clothes she had on. "What's up?" she asked. Excitedly he told her that it was the same date he gave her first skating lesson, and he wanted to go to the skating rink and celebrate. Summer also became excited and she thought, Wow, we have not been there in a while. It would be so fun. No, I definitely can't tell him tonight. One more night of fun and I will tell him tomorrow.

They went to the skating rink and they both skated like pros, drawing attention from those all around them. The people cleared the floor and watched the amazing duo go at it. Summer felt like the queen of the ball and was so glad Jamie taught her to skate. Things seemed perfect once more as they twirled the floor together. The crowd cheered them on. Summer skated away in front of Jamie to show off her special spin which he had taught her. The spin was perfectly done. Summer was expecting more of the same from the crowd with more of their cheers and raving, but to her surprise all she heard was gossiping horrified sounds mixed with screaming. She turned to look behind her. Jamie lay collapsed on the cold ice with the loud music she never heard. She skated to him as fast as she could, screaming his name. He was unresponsive. They stopped the music and everyone heard Summer yelling for someone to call 911.

Jamie woke up in a hospital bed with a throbbing head and an aching body like he had never felt before. He turned to Summer, who was beside him in a chair pulled up to his bed. "What happened?" he requested to know. "You collapsed at the skating rink." "What's wrong with me?" Jamie asked in a groggy, medicated voice. She looked up at him sadly. "I don't know," she replied. Then she lowered her head in shame. Unable to look him in his eyes, she told him the doctor would be in shortly. The doctor came in and spoke with Jamie and his wife. He told them he needed to run some tests before he told them anything for sure. He assured Jamie that he would be in the hospital for a while. "It appears that you have walking pneumonia. I was informed the rescue brought you in from the ice-skating rink. I think the cold from the ice set you off. You probably had it for a while and didn't even know it, walking pneumonia is tricky that way," the doctor informed them. "It's going to take about two days for me to get all the tests done on you. I'm going to leave you in the hands of our good nurses to get the tests started. I will be speaking with you again in a couple of days," the doctor said as he exited the hospital room. For the next two days Summer stayed in the hospital with Jamie. She never once mentioned her having HIV; again she felt it was not the right time. When the doctor made his way to Jamie's room, the stern look on his face made Summer nervous. The doctor asked Jamie if he wanted Summer to step out of the room before he told him of the test results. Jamie told him no and that he had nothing to hide from his wife. "Okay, then I will begin. Well it's official, you do have walking pneumonia. There is another problem, though, that may have caused you to have been more susceptible to get the pneumonia. Jamie, you have AIDS." Summer was shocked to hear the news. She spoke up even before Jamie. "AIDS, are you SURE? AIDS? Not HIV?" The doctor answered her, "Yes he had HIV, but HIV untreated can turn into AIDS very quickly in some people. Some people's immune systems just aren't strong enough to handle it long." Jamie listened to his wife and the doctor talk back and forth as if he were watching a dream. He thought if he didn't talk he would soon wake up from the nightmare. "Jamie," the doctor called to get his attention, "I wish you had come to us sooner, your blood count is very low. I want to give you a blood transfusion tomorrow and get an AIDS counselor in to speak with you in the morning; also, I want to get you started on some meds immediately." The doctor told Jamie these things and he never said a word. Summer looked at Jamie and his eyes were wide open so he wasn't sleep. Why wasn't he saying anything? Why wasn't he asking questions? she wondered. "What's wrong with him, Doctor?" "Could be the medicine he is on, could be the shock of the news.

Give him a little time to process things," he said just before walking out of the room. Summer was fearful being left in the room alone with Jamie. It was silent with Summer being afraid to talk and Jamie still thinking he was asleep. The silence soon became too much for Summer so she called Jamie's name. "Summer," he called back. "Yes?" "Tell me it was a nightmare." Tears welled up in her eyes as she told him she would love to tell him that but she couldn't. "How, how is this even possible? This can't be possible," Jamie ranted on. "They need to do the test again," he spoke with authority. Summer knew that her time was up. No more putting off talking to Jamie. She put her hand on his hand to calm him. "No, my dear, there is no need for a second test. I have something to tell you and I'm sorry I couldn't, well didn't, tell you sooner. Jamie, I have to say this before I cry so forgive me for saying it fast. I had an affair. It's been like a year ago. It only happened once. I found out a few months ago the guy was HIV positive and I got tested and now so am I." Jamie squinted his eyes in disbelief. He jerked his hand from beneath hers and he looked away. When his hand left hers, she felt a detachment that would never be joined again. "I never meant to hurt you," she cried. Tears now streamed from his face, which had not happened in his whole adult life. He turned his head further to the wall so they wouldn't be seen, but it was too late. "Are you in pain?" she asked, for he had never looked back at her, but he did respond. "The tears are not for the physical pain. I loved you, Summer," he told her with deep emotion. "I never cheated on you and I never thought you could cheat on me. Layla told me and I fired her for lying on my wife. I never even mentioned it to you because I trusted you so much."

Summer was breaking on the inside listening to him. The unbearable part was him facing the wall. "Could you please look at me?" She cried out for his compassion but he didn't turn, and she could no longer feel the warmth he once had for her. Jamie stopped talking. Summer cried more, saying "please look at me," but he couldn't. The nurses came in the room. "Mr. Garnett, it's time for your new medication the doctor has put you on." Jamie continued looking at the wall and said, "You need to leave." One of the nurses responded, "But we really need to give you this medicine." "I wasn't talking to you. Summer...," he called her name. "Yes, Jamie," she asked. "You need to leave," he told her with a cold voice that came straight from the heart. The nurses were stunned that he was putting his wife out, but not as stunned as Summer; she stood silently as shivers ran up her spine. She wanted to tell Jamie he couldn't mean that, but she couldn't speak. She feared if she said one word, she would cry out loud in the hospital and would be thrown out. She backed herself to the door while staring at Jamie. She prayed on the inside that he would turn around so she could see his eyes. Look at me; look in my eyes like you always have with that caring, concern, and compassion. She cried on the inside wishing she were brave enough to speak it aloud, but knowing she was undeserving of any of it. She made it into the hallway, still looking in; the nurse told her she was sorry, she was going to have to close the door. She nodded in agreement but still she stood there. The nurse started closing the door slowly, hoping that she would walk away, but she stayed. Just before clicking the door shut in her face, the nurse whispered "sorry."

Summer found herself standing in front of her car

door in the packed hospital parking lot. Her mind was so traumatized she did not recall the walk downstairs. She did not want to leave Jamie, but he gave her no choice. She got in her car and started driving home. The drive home was difficult. She could barely see through all the water that kept filling her eyes. It was much like driving on a rainy day, but on this day the sun shined bright on the outside but Summer did not notice. All she felt was gloom and darkness as she used her fingers to wipe away the pouring tears. As she drove on, she looked ahead and thought she saw a car driving forward on her side of the road. Summer panicked. She was on a bridge; there was traffic to her left and water to her right. She did not know which way to turn, but she did know a head-on collision could kill her. If she moved the car to the left lane that could still be a head-on collision, but if she drove her car into the ocean, she figured she would surely drown. Scared and alone, she decided to stop her car in the middle of the road and just take the hit. She covered her eyes and shook like a single leaf blowing in the wind on a windy day. As her eyes remained covered for a while, she noticed the silence all around her. Why wasn't she dead? she wondered. She should be dead, she thought. She removed her hands from her eyes and looked around. She was parked on the bridge alone. There was no other traffic—not beside her, behind her, or in front of her. There never was. Her mind had only created it all, from the traumatic experience. She began screaming and crying aloud. "Oh God! Now I'm going crazy, please help me!" Summer wished the accident could have been real. She felt she deserved it for what she had done to Jamie. As soon as that thought crossed her mind, a car pulled up behind her. All Summer could make out from looking through the car mirror with her watery eyes was a bright glowing figure. She figured they would be blowing their horn at them soon, but they didn't. A woman stepped out of the car and came up to Summer's window. She saw Summer, torn and confused. Summer rolled her window down and the sight of the woman seemed to comfort her. The woman never asked Summer what was wrong; she only gave her encouraging words and told her whatever the problem, maybe one day it would all be okay. Summer was not sure how that was possible, but still the peace that came with the elderly stranger gave Summer the courage to make it home. When Summer got home her mind fell on the lady she'd seen. She wondered why the woman was so nice and why she bothered stopping at all. She could have just driven around. Summer felt that if the mystery woman had not showed up she never would have made it home, so she considered the lady to have been her guardian angel, which was just what she needed on a night such as the one she was living. Also, the whole situation gave her something else to focus on, which she deeply needed to keep herself from exploding.

Summer had been staying away like Jamie requested. She knew the pain from his rejection was too much for her to bear.

Day one after Summer was thrown out of her husband's hospital room by Jamie himself, Summer woke up raising her head from a tear-stained pillow. Drained from a night of emotional distress, she just sat straight up in bed expressing no emotion. After a night of stress and a morning of pure sadness, Summer eventually threw her covers back and hopped out of bed. Her sadness had turned to anger and bitterness. She had been through many stages, such as depression, isolation, and now she had hit anger, and she figured she would never make it to acceptance. She dressed herself, then went down to the kitchen and prepared breakfast. She was cracking eggs into a bowl when one missed and hit the floor. This wasn't the first time this had ever happened to Summer, but today it made her furious. She kicked one of the legs of a chair at her kitchen table. She kicked it so hard the chair fell to the ground. The chair bumped her a bit on the way down. This made Summer jump back, bumping the kitchen table, which held the bowl of eggs. The bowl was thrust off of the table and onto the floor, where the eggs splattered not only the floor but also onto Summer's bare feet. The whole incident with the eggs spilling on her bare feet reminded her of Jamie. He always told her to wear shoes or slippers in the kitchen, but Summer barely obeyed that request. Tears began to come to her eyes, but she refused to let them fall. She yanked her forearm up to her face, wiping her eyes with her sleeve. Her face frowned as anger welled up over the tears. Summer was angry at herself, Summer was angry at the situation, and a small part of her was even angry at Jamie for throwing her out of his hospital room.

Summer grabbed some paper towels and wiped the eggs from the floor and off her feet. She set the chair she had kicked over back up. She washed the bowl out and started to prepare the eggs once more. Summer felt she could not let the eggs defeat her like so much had already done; she thought to herself she would finish the task and she would do it well just so she could feel like she had control over something in her life. Summer finished cooking, then she sat down at the table and began to feast over the pretty burnt eggs, which weren't even her favorite breakfast food. After she finished her burnt eggs, she went to pour herself more orange juice. As she poured the juice into the empty cup without holding the cup, the heaviness of the juice made the cup flip over. Juice was all over the table. Summer left it there. She went to her room, got in her bed with her clothes still on; she covered her head and lay there all night. If breakfast time was that hard, she dared not face the rest of the day, and there ended day one.

Day two, Summer woke and reached for the phone. She called Jamie's room number at the hospital. A nurse answered the phone. Summer asked to speak to her husband. The nurse told Summer to hold on the line while she relayed the message to Mr. Garnett. The nurse came back to the phone and told Summer that Jamie Garnett did not wish to take calls from her. The nurse appeared to be projecting an attitude towards Summer. It was really not the day for Summer to hear anyone talking to her in such a manner. Summer frowned her face and hardened her voice with a stern, nasty pitch that was sure to reach the nurse. "First of all, who do you think you are speaking to in that tone? I am MRS. Garnett! I have the right to speak with him. I don't know why you are even in the room answering his phone. You need better remember I'm his wife, you're his nurse," Summer ranted on to the nurse. It seemed that she was trying to convince herself that she still had a place in Jamie's life. The nurse took the whole conversation to have been very strange and pointless. The nurse said, "Look, Mrs. Garnett, no offense to you, but I'm just doing my job, and if you had been doing yours, your husband wouldn't be telling me right now to hang up this phone on you." The last thing Summer heard before a dial tone was the nurse laughing softly. The nurse said what she said and then hung up the phone, leaving Summer on the other end still holding the phone to her ear. Summer hung up the phone and headed to the bathroom for a shower. After dressing in jeans and a tee shirt, Summer had a bowl of cereal and got in her car. She was going to the hospital whether Jamie liked it or not. She did go to the hospital, but when she arrived she was too afraid to get out of her car. She didn't know what had come over her, but she was scared. Also, she felt kind of stupid for what she'd said to the nurse.

She had a perfect view of Jamie's room window, but his room was so high up she could see nothing but the curtains moving occasionally. Strangely enough this did give her a little comfort.

The decision was hard, but Summer decided to respect Jamie's wishes and she did not go in. She told herself that she was respecting his wishes and her head believed it, but her heart knew that she had lost her courage. She hoped that he just needed time to cool off and he would soon forgive her. Summer drove off and went all the way to her hometown. She arrived at her usual place: the greenest park in the world with the old apple tree. It was not a cold day, it was not a warm day. It was much like the way Summer felt on the inside: undecided as to which way she should go. She took out her blanket and walked to the apple tree. She lay beneath it and took comfort in its shade. There were many people at the park on this Saturday. She looked around and envied most of what she saw. A man and woman holding hands laughing out loud walked right past her. Always across from her was another couple engaging in a picnic with their jackets on. That did bring a smile to Summer's face as she remembered the freezing cold picnic. Thanksgiving dinner that she and Jamie shared as they wore even heavier coats. Summer closed her eyes as she lay on the blanket so she couldn't see any more. She tried hard to fall asleep so she couldn't think any more. She had hoped a sweet dream would come and take her away, back to the past when she and Jamie's life was perfect again; she did eventually fall asleep but she did not get her wish. No sweet dreams were permitted—only nightmares. She woke up angry and said out loud, "If I wanted a nightmare I would have stayed awake." Summer stood, snatched up her blanket, and bitterly walked back to her car, where she drove home and ended her night.

Day three, Summer woke up and got herself ready to go to the hospital again. She drove there telling herself this time she would go inside the hospital, and when she arrived she did go inside. She just didn't go upstairs to Jamie's room. She stayed in the downstairs lobby for hours watching families come and go. Even though she was not in Jamie's room with him, she still found comfort in being so close to him. Being in the same building somehow made her feel that she was there for him. As she sat in the lobby, she saw an elderly couple walk into the hospital. She figured they both had to be in their eighties. They came in holding hands. They went to the front desk to get visitor stickers. Summer was amazed they were visitors and not patients. She watched the two of them. The elderly woman walked towards the gift shop. She went inside and Summer continued to watch her through the glass. She came out with flowers for whomever they were visiting. Her husband saw the flowers and came up to her saying to her how thoughtful a woman he had married, and they joined hands again and walked off together. At first Summer thought the sight was beautiful. The man had reminded her of how Jamie always said such sweet things about her. Then her heart was soon saddened. Now she knew that Jamie's thoughts of her had been torn and tarnished. No more was she the sweet, thoughtful wife. Summer thought more of the elderly couple and it only made her think more. Even if Jamie would forgive her and they got back together the two of them would never grow old together; well, she thought, with this disease on the both of us it is definitely not likely.

Summer used her cell phone and called Jamie's room again. This time she got no answer at all. She told herself Jamie was answering no one's calls just so he could avoid her. "No, he don't want me here," Summer said softly with teary eyes as she stood to leave the hospital. She returned back home and all of her sadness flooded her heart and leaked out from her eyes. Being without Jamie was breaking her heart. She had never felt so alone. The same as the last two nights, she ended the third night alone.

On the fourth day Summer got her nerve up to go back to the hospital, and this time she would make it all the way upstairs. She wanted to be there for Jamie. When she went to the front desk at the hospital, they gave her a mask to cover her face. "No entrance without a mask"—she was told it was for Jamie's safety to keep the germs away from him. Summer walked into Jamie's room without knocking. She figured when he heard it was her at the door, he would yell for her to get out. To her surprise Jamie was in no condition to yell, but there was someone else in the room who could. When Summer opened Jamie's hospital room door, she had a double devastation. First of all Jamie was just lying in bed with no movement. Then before she could walk with him out, sitting back in a corner sat Jamie's mother! Jamie's mom stood to her feet and yelled at Summer to leave her son's room. Summer was thrown off guard to see her and was shocked to hear her yelling at her inside of a hospital. Summer's first response was to shush her so she would not disturb Jamie. This action only upset Jamie's mom more. She yelled at Summer again to leave the room. Summer closed the room as she saw nurses approaching. "Please, Mrs. Garnett, if you don't lower your voice, they will throw us both out." The room door then opened again. It was a nurse asking was there a problem. Jamie's mom spoke up in a calm, friendly voice, saying, "Oh no, dear, there is nothing wrong, everything is just fine. I just got a little excited to see my daughter-in-law. I will lower my voice," she said as she took her seat. The nurse said, "Okay, please do keep the noise down so the patient will not be disturbed." The nurse closed the door behind her and Summer walked to Jamie's bedside. He lay in pain, grunting every few seconds. He would not respond to her at all. "What happened to him? I have been gone for only a few days and he looks like this?" Summer asked. Jamie's mom walked over to her. "You are what happened to him. You and your poison," Mrs. Garnett said in a hushed voice. "My son called me the day he threw you out of here and told me all about how you deceived him. You never loved him," Jamie's mom told Summer.

"That's not true, I do love him. I always loved him and

I always will. Did Jamie tell you I didn't love him? Did he really think that, huh?"

"Don't worry about what my son said or what he thinks. You lost that privilege. I don't know what you are doing here in this room. In this hospital at all. Didn't my son throw you out? So you were not only posing to him, but now you want to disobey his wishes?!" said Jamie's mom to Summer. Summer became overwhelmed and teary-eyed; she didn't respond back to Jamie's mom. She just looked down at Jamie. She looked at him lying on the bed frail and weak. Oxygen was on his face and he was too ill to speak to her. She stepped out of the room. Summer tried to ignore Jamie's mom and focused on him. Angry and confused, she went to the nurses' station and demanded to see Jamie's doctor. She was told he was not in the hospital, but he was scheduled to be there in about an hour to do rounds. The nurses told Summer they would contact the doctor and see if he could make Jamie's room his first round. Summer went back to the room to sit with Jamie. She tried to speak with him, but only got grunts instead, and the grunts she was unsure if they were for her or the pain. Summer focused on Jamie, and his mom continued to sit in the corner, watching and grunting as well. Those grunts Summer was sure were aimed towards her, but Summer refused to leave her husband, and Mrs. Garnett refused to leave her son, so they both stayed. The sight of Jamie sick and there was nothing she could do to him became too much for her to bear. She stepped in the hallway and vigorously passed the floor waiting for the doctor. After a while, a nurse came to her and told her that the doctor would like to see her in a room down the hall. Summer was ready; she walked quickly behind the nurse. She walked into the room and angrily attacked the doctor with questions. "What's wrong with him? It's only been a few days since I have seen him. How did he get so sick?" she demanded to know. "He can't even talk to me and he looks like he is hurting," Summer said as she continued to inform the doctor of what she had witnessed. The doctor told Summer that Jamie's body rejected the AIDS medication. "It does not work for everyone, and unfortunately he happens to be one of the few. I'm sorry, Miss Garnett, but Jamie's immune system is just too low to fight the pneumonia." The doctor told Summer this sadly.

"What does this mean? If he is too weak to fight it, then how do we help him?" Summer asked in denial.

"All we can do now is try and make him comfortable," he responded.

"How much time? A year? A few months?"

"No, I hate to say it, but he may only have a few more days, maybe less." Summer ran out of his office and down the hall to a restroom, where she cried alone.

She gathered her composure and dared herself to be strong for Jamie. She went back to his room and stayed by his side, despite glares from his mom.

A week later Jamie was still alive to the doctor's surprise. Summer had stayed at the hospital the entire time since her return. The poor nurses had much to deal with. Every time the nurses would come in to reposition him or anything she would demand the chance to help them, and so would Jamie's mother. A nurse came up with the idea that they took turns helping. Jamie still could not communicate. His eyes would pop open and stare into corners, but never would they focus on a person.

Night came and Summer was still with Jamie. His mom went home. She said to her son she would be back early the next day, as she kissed him on his forehead. She just walked past Summer, rolling her eyes as she exited the hospital room. During the night Jamie's pains had worsened to the point where they had to up his medication. Summer was informed that an extra dose of morphine would keep Jamie out of pain, but it could also mean that he might not make it through the night.

Time passed slowly as his grunts from pain increased through the night. The medicine was not helping much. Jamie's body shook and all the nurses could say to Summer was it was the medicine. Summer's heart ached as badly as Jamie's body pained. She took Jamie's hand and leaned towards him. "I'm sorry," she sobbed. "This was all my fault. I know 'I'm sorry' is not good enough, but it is all I have to give. Please know that if I could go back in time that I would erase it all. There would be no affair, so there would be no AIDS, there would be no pain. Forgive me," she begged repeatedly. Suddenly Jamie's hand that had lain limp all week gripped her hand tightly. It stopped her tears from rolling for a moment. "Does this mean you forgive me? Jamie, thank you, for your love, compassion, and forgiveness," she sobbed. The machines hooked to Jamie beeped loudly and his hand began to loosen slowly from hers as the line on the monitor grew large and wavy. The nurses ran in the room, then the line on the monitor ran flat. Silence entered the room. Jamie was dead. The silence ended as Summer's scream echoed through the hospital. After a moment a couple of nurses took her down to the chapel to mourn. Summer walked in the chapel alone. She lit three candles and turned off the lights in the room. She placed herself in a seat where she just sat staring at the lights in a paralyzed state. She was in complete shock at how this all happened so fast. She wondered so many things as she sat alone in the chapel for hours. Summer wondered why this had happened to Jamie and not her since she was the cause of the problem. Then she wondered was she dreaming, but she quickly decided she must be awake because she had never felt such unbearable pain in a dream before. The longer she sat thinking, the more candles went out one by one until she was only down to one.

Thoughts of how Jason had told her it could be a secret that could never hurt anyone if they both stayed quiet about it. She wondered why she'd listened because now that one moment of bliss had cost her everything.

As that last light flickered and dimmed completely, leaving her in pitch dark, the statement rang in her ears repeatedly: *No one ever has to know.*

Printed in the United States
By Bookmasters